ALANIS KING

3 PLAYS

IF JESUS MET NANABUSH
THE TOMMY PRINCE STORY
BORN BUFFALO

ALANIS KING

THREE PLAYS

FIFTH
HOUSE

Published in Canada by Red Deer Press,
195 Allstate Parkway, Markham, Ontario L3R 4T8

Published in the United States by Red Deer Press,
311 Washington Street, Brighton, Massachusetts 02135

www.reddeerpress.com

10 9 8 7 6 5 4 3 2 1

Red Deer Press acknowledges with thanks the Ontario Arts Council for their support
of our publishing program. We acknowledge the financial support of the
Government of Canada through the Canada Book Fund (CBF) for our publishing activities.

ONTARIO ARTS COUNCIL
CONSEIL DES ARTS DE L'ONTARIO
an Ontario government agency
un organisme du gouvernement de l'Ontario

Library and Archives Canada Cataloguing in Publication
King, Alanis, author
Three plays / Alanis King.
Contents: If Jesus met Nanabush – The Tommy Prince story – Born Buffalo.
ISBN 978-1-927083-32-1 (pbk.)
I. Title.
PS8621.I5558T47 2015   C812'.6   C2015-902515-X

Publisher Cataloging-in-Publication Data (U.S)
King, Alanis.
Three plays / Alanis King.
[148] pages : cm.
Notes: If Jesus met Nanabush – The Tommy Prince story – Born Buffalo.
ISBN: 978-1-92708-332-1 (pbk.)
1. American drama – 21st century. I. Title. II. King, Alanis. If Jesus met Nanabush. III.
King, Alanis. Tommy Prince story. IV. King, Alanis. Born Buffalo.
812.6 dc23   PS3611.I64T4 2015

Also published in electronic formats.

Cover and text design by Tanya Montini
Printed in Canada by Friesens Corporation

MIX
Paper from
responsible sources
FSC® C016245
FSC
www.fsc.org

CONTENTS

1. A Note About The Author IX

2. If Jesus Met Nanabush 1

3. The Tommy Prince Story 55

4. Born Buffalo 113

A NOTE ABOUT THE AUTHOR

Growing up surrounded by music, dance and storytelling, Alanis King turned to drama early, not only as a way to express herself, but to explore the rich heritage of her community. In fact, it was here at the Wikwemikong Unceded Indian Reserve on Manitoulin Island that Alanis embraced her community's vibrant oral traditions, ageless stories filled with grand characters and deities as magical as any found in the Western canon. In talking about her work, Alanis notes: "I'm not interested in teaching or presenting Shakespeare or Molière because we have our own classics that we have to explore: creation stories, myths, histories. We have lots of writing to do, lots of plays to do that have not been out there. It's in our oral traditions so we need to remain connected to the elders."

Playwright and director Alanis King has quietly become a force in Native North American drama. Born into the Odawa Nation, Alanis became the first Aboriginal woman to graduate from the National Theatre School of Canada. She is a past Artistic Director of the Debajehmujig Theatre Group and the Native Earth Performing Arts in Toronto. She was also Artistic Director at the Saskatchewan Native Theatre where she taught risk-prone inner city youth life skills through drama. King has also produced, toured, directed and developed a wide range of plays in many First Nation communities across the continent.

To date her critically acclaimed plays also include *Manitoulin Incident, Bye Bye Beneshe, Song of Hiawatha: An Anishnaabec Adaptation, Order of Good Cheer, Gegwah, Lovechild, Artshow,* and *Heartdwellers*.

Like all good drama, the three works collected here spring from the community and experiences of the playwright, but in such good hands the results are universal. As Alanis concludes, "we create for ourselves, but all are welcome."

IF JESUS
MET NANABUSH

If Jesus Met Nanabush was workshopped at Playwright's Workshop Montreal after winning a student playwriting contest in 1992. It was first produced by Debajehmujig Theatre Group at Pontiac School Auditorium, Wikwemikong, in October 1993 with the following:

Directed by Anne Anglin
Set and Costume Design by Karen Jones

The cast were:
Nanabush . . . . .Clayton Odjig
Jesus . . . . Alon Nashman
Kwewag . . . . Sharon King
Stage Manager . . . . Jeffrey Trudeau
Assistant Stage Manager,
Traditional Singer, Waiter . . . . .Craig Trudeau
Sound Operator . . . . Elizabeth Pasternak

The author wishes to extend her deep gratitude to Dylan Dominic Odjig who came into being during the rehearsal of this play and went to the premiere two weeks later. A special thanks also to Paul Thompson, Clayton Odjig, Elizabeth Pasternak, Anne Anglin, Sharon King, Alon Nashman, and the entire cast, crew and Debajehmujig production team.

PRODUCTION NOTES

This one-act play is initially set at the Champion of Champions
Pow-Wow on Six Nations and then takes a journey across Turtle
Island on the pow-wow trail.

Nanabush is the Anishnaabe name for the trickster, who is half man,
half spirit, holds all the strengths of the Great Spirit, yet holds all
the weakness of man. In this production he is a male fancy dancer.
Nanabush was responsible for naming all life and has the ability to
transform into other entities including a coyote. Kwewag is a female
deity, and therefore also has the ability to transform. In the play she
is a Pow-Wow Dance Judge, a Winter Woman, a Biker Chick and a
Cleaning Lady. Since Kwewag is from the realm of magical beings
she and Nanabush are familiar with each other.

Anishnaabemowin is the language utilized in the play.

CAST OF CHARACTERS

Nanabush, the only human to hold all the powers of the Great Spirit yet too, all the weaknesses of mankind. Nanabush is commonly known as a trickster.

Jesus (Godfrey), the only son of God from the Holy Bible.

Kwewag, a Native female deity.

Singer, a lead singer for a champion drum group.

This play is dedicated to my son, Dominic Odjig, a soldier and a new daddy to be.

SCENE 1

Kwewag is standing expectant in a spot of light.
Gradually we hear a helicopter beat which
intensifies until there's blackout. In darkness
the drum starts and the Singer and the other
singers begin the shake-dance song. Kwewag
is now seen singing along but by herself. When
it is not her turn to sing she dances along; her
focus is on Nanabush. The lights come up full as
in a daylight outdoors setting. Nanabush, in his
twenties and a fancy dancer, enters to the beat of
the drum. He dances, four times through, never
missing the fast-trick stop. Then on the final beat,
he stops right on time before the woman, center
stage, arms up, legs apart and hollers loudly.
They smile. She takes her pencil and paper and,
as a Dance Judge, goes to hand in her place
picks. Jesus, in his twenties, walks on wearing
a long white robe, long hair and yet looks too
young for a full beard. The Singer takes in his
dress and exits laughing.

JESUS:

Does dancing like that always make you sweat?

NANABUSH:

Only if I really like the song.

JESUS:

Oh.

NANABUSH:

That or first prize is a thousand bucks.

JESUS:

A thousand ... bucks ... buck. You don't mean a deer do you?

NANABUSH:

I'd dance for that too. But I mean money.

JESUS:

Money?

NANABUSH:

Yes.

JESUS:

You dance for, er, money?

NANABUSH:

Yes.

JESUS:

I'm sorry, I thought you danced for rain or the sun or
something. Where does the money come from?

NANABUSH:

From whoever puts on the pow-wow.

JESUS:

Pow-wow. What's a pow-wow?

NANABUSH:

What you see here. Didn't you know that when you came in?

JESUS:

Came in?

NANABUSH:

When you walked through the gate. Admissions.

JESUS:

No, I didn't come in there.

NANABUSH:

How'd you come in then? Chopper? Oh, I know. You hopped the fence. Security!

JESUS:

No, no, I just appeared. Showed up. I heard the drum beating, so I got here.

NANABUSH:

Yeah! Me too. Pow-wow's good for the soul. Anybody could dance or sing. *(rattles his bustles like a butterfly)* I like it here. It's a good pow-wow. The Champion of Champions. Can't beat that. Good slogan anyway. You live around here?

JESUS:

No.

NANABUSH:

Me neither. But I was here last year. Took first.

JESUS:

Took first what?

NANABUSH:

First prize.

JESUS:

Oh ... "A thousand bucks"!

NANABUSH:

You got it. And maybe I will again this time. Seeing as there's only four of us and Craig can't dance. No rhythm.

JESUS:

Who's Craig?

NANABUSH:

The one with the yellow bandana on his head. He likes to hide his blond hair.

JESUS:

Blond hair?

NANABUSH:

Yeah. He's no Indian but he wants to be.

JESUS:

Why would anyone want to be an Indian?

NANABUSH:

Hey, come on now. You're asking me that?

JESUS:
>If he's not an Indian why would he want to be one? And wear a yellow bandana to cover his yellow hair?

NANABUSH:
>For the women.

JESUS:
>Do they know he's not an Indian?

NANABUSH:
>Of course.

JESUS:
>The women know he's not an Indian. And the women know his yellow bandana is hiding his yellow hair. Then why does everyone let him be an Indian?

NANABUSH:
>He's not. I said he can't dance.

JESUS:
>Does he know that?

NANABUSH:
>Obviously not. He wants first prize. But he's not going to get it.

The drum starts, then the singing. Nanabush begins to dance.

NANABUSH:
>Come on! Intertribal. Let's dance.

JESUS:
>No.

NANABUSH:
Why not?

JESUS:
I'm not an Indian either.

Nanabush laughs, retreats upstage, and dances until he disappears. The daylight dims to a single spotlight on Jesus. The drum beat switches to a low flying helicopter beat which underscores the following:

JESUS:
I'm an Israelite. Hot and dry. Light and shadow. Like the sun that shines his bustles that brought me. I've landed here to complete the final journey left. My only purpose left. To find my living equal. Failing will not lose the masses, only the dozen followers, for in my search I am sure of only one thing. The Earth beneath my feet is bubbling and shaking its head in red alert. This is it. This is wholly venture. Process for keeps.

He exits, ducking his head from a big wind just as a person might when boarding a helicopter. He's gone. The sound stops. Kwewag has been standing on stage listening. With a fancy move, she makes the light come up to full daylight again. Nanabush appears carrying his bustles, a trophy, a suitcase, and an envelope. He's wearing angora leggings, moccasins and bells around each calf. The Singer has been helping him pack the car with his bustles and trophy. His tape player blasts out Steve Miller's "Rockin' Me Baby".

KWEWAG:
(she rushes to Nanabush) It's him! I know it.

NANABUSH:
How can you be sure?

KWEWAG:
I heard him. You're his equal. You're alive.

SINGER:
Just ask him.

NANABUSH:
Could be a fake.

SINGER:
A hippie — *(laughing)*

NANABUSH:
— he looks like one.

KWEWAG:
No. He's him. You're you. That's it. I'm outta here. Be careful.
We'll be nearby.

She exits with the Singer.

*At this point Jesus appears. Nanabush, singing along, senses someone
behind him.*

NANABUSH:
Jesus! You scared me.

JESUS:
I'm sorry. I didn't mean to.

NANABUSH:
Look. *(points to the trophy)* First prize. *(picks up the envelope,
displays a wad of twenties)* Thousand bucks! *(he fans the bills)*

JESUS:

    (laughs) So you did it. What did yellow bandana do?

NANABUSH:

    You mean yellow bandit. Fourth.

JESUS:

    Fourth! Maybe I should have danced.

NANABUSH:

    You know what I'm going to do with all this money?
    (pause) I'm going to go buy me a six-pack. And put gas in
    my car. Then I'm off. I'm heading south. South where the
    big competition is. If I win down there I'm gonna buy me a
    new pair of bustles. Then I'll go to Albuquerque. Seventy-
    five fancy feather dancers in my division alone. That's
    competition! Not like here. I'll dance circles around each
    one of them. *(stomps his feet triumphantly, bells are heard)*
    Ever been south? Desert country, some of it.

JESUS:

    Where abouts is south?

NANABUSH:

    Oklahoma is the first stop. Thirty-two hours. My Mustang is
    good as long as I give her gas. So whatdya say? You want to
    go? Split costs fifty-fifty.

JESUS:

    To Oklahoma. Then south. Desert country. There's wild animals
    in the desert. Wild coyotes. I was bit by one. It made me delirious.

NANABUSH:
Well there's no desert in Oklahoma. So there's no wild coyotes either. There are wild Foxes and Kiowas though. That's why I want to stop there. Spend time with some buddies. Nice guys. *(imitates their American accent)* We'd all like you to have a real good time, y'all.

JESUS:
Oh. So when you leaving?

NANABUSH:
Right now. Um beh.

JESUS:
Go ahead. I'll catch up to you later —

Jesus exits.

NANABUSH:
(facing where Jesus exited) You don't come now you'll never catch up to me. But suit yourself. See ya around. Somewhere down the trail. Hey! What's your name?!

Nanabush exits. The following audio syncs with a show of North American pow-wows, a trail of highways, sunsets and rest stops. Nanabush is driving a vintage Mustang Ford on an interstate highway in America. Picturesque landscapes of endless cornfields, mesas in badlands country, then the desert and wild horses and ranches. He has been driving non-stop at top speed to make it in time to register as a dancer at the next big competition pow-wow. First you hear static of a car radio being tuned until we hear the Rolling Stones' "Sympathy for the Devil."

NANABUSH:

> Hitchhiker! At this hour! Hee hee. *(stopping the car)* Jesus —
> look who we have here!

JESUS:

> Still headin' south?

NANABUSH:

> Hop in.

JESUS:

> Yeah. I changed my mind. I thought I'd flag you down. With
> this yellow bandana.

NANABUSH:

> So how'd you know I'd be coming along here? At this time?
> And you've never seen my car. And how did you wind up in
> Utah ahead of me? And where the hell are your bags?! And
> what's your name?!

JESUS:

> *(holding a map)* Based on your mention of this car's gas
> consumption I calculated it to be a '68 Mustang. And since you
> like the color purple so much, I recognized the paint job. And
> there's only one interstate from here to Oklahoma — if you're
> travelling south. And I can't be bothered carrying baggage. If I
> need something, I'll find it. And as for my name ... I thought
> you knew. But since you ask, the name's Godfrey.

SCENE 2

The next afternoon. The setting is a small-town tavern somewhere in the very center of America. The jukebox is playing "Devil Went Down to Georgia." Godfrey is alone at a table. Nanabush enters. Two draft beers are on the table. The bar is dimly lit, has sawdust on the floor — a real cowboy place, wood beams and barnwood walls are hung with old horse saddles and horse tack. Smoking is permitted. A Biker Chick enters, goes to the jukebox and makes a selection, Billy Idol's "Rebel Yell." She turns and stares at Jesus while pulling out a shiny whiskey flask.

BIKER CHICK:

Well I'm thirsty. *(she takes a swig)* Has anyone ever told you you look like Jesus?

Jesus looks around making sure she's referring to him before he answers.

JESUS:

Uh — no — not lately.

BIKER CHICK:

Well I don't know why the heck not. I mean, look at yourself, anyone walking around in a long robe and a beard — come on now — honey — really? Is that your own beard or did you buy that at the five and dime?

JESUS:

Oh it's mine alright.

BIKER CHICK:

Oh great. I just get released from Hell's Angels prison and the first person I run into is a Saviour. Save me — *save me*! From the wolves and wild creatures who wish to devour me daily. Hah!!

JESUS:

I cannot save you. You must save yourself.

BIKER CHICK:

You cannot save me. I must save — oh that's good. How about you? Better watch your own butt, don't you know what happens to you? Watch this town, those Angels would hang you by the balls just for looking different, I know they would me ... if I had any.

*She lights up a smoke and, scrutinizing Jesus, moves to the music.
She advances toward him to offer her whiskey flask.*

BIKER CHICK:
I'm thirsty.

JESUS:
(turning his back to her) I'm just waiting on a friend — he'll be
right along.

She retreats to the washroom.

Nanabush enters.

NANABUSH:
The mechanic at the station says about another half hour. I
thought that tire would've lasted the remaining three hundred
miles. Tires are cheap in the south. But still. *(he bangs his glass
on the table)* It pops off! Did you see how it sped right past us?
Like I wasn't going fast enough for it. Zoom! Mind of its own.
Veers into the divided highway. Whizzes up on the other side.
Checks that side of the road out for awhile then dips back in,
hits a rock, flies, spins and stops. One last quiver then BAM!
(bangs glass again) Put that one in your dance step. *(he drinks)*

JESUS:
I must say you handled the vehicle with the utmost care.

NANABUSH:
Shit man, I just hit the brakes! You're the one. Just quietly
watching this solo speeding tire just zoom by us as if that's
normal. As if it was supposed to happen. Geez, I don't know.

JESUS:
Seemed to me the only option was to stop our moving vehicle as safely as possible, flag someone down to take us to the nearest telephone, call a tow truck, retrieve the tire and wait for the repair. *(the Biker Chick re-enters.)* Since you say you've lost the spare.

NANABUSH:
Yes, that's evident isn't it.

Nanabush notices the Biker Chick walking by their table. He gets up and trails after her.

NANABUSH:
Hi how are ya. Hi how are ya. You hoo. You need a ride. Mmmm hmmm. Mmmm hmmm.

JESUS:
Too much perfume. Reek. Jeans way too tight. And all those colors on her face.

Nanabush has rejoined Jesus at the table and Biker Chick has made her exit in disgust.

JESUS:
Must have come from a circus. Despite of what she said.

NANABUSH:
No. No. That chick was on her way. Somewhere. If you had taken a guzzle of her whiskey flask. We'd still be with her.

JESUS:
I dislike whiskey very much. The smell of it makes me want to vomit.

NANABUSH:

So what! There are certain sacrifices you got to make when you're in the company of women.

JESUS:

I'm not going to force myself to do something I don't want to and you can't pressure me either.

NANABUSH:

Fake it.

JESUS:

How?

NANABUSH:

Put the bottle to your lips. Like this. *(pulls out the whiskey flask)* Tip the bottle back, hold it for three seconds. Swallow. Then smile.

JESUS:

Hey! That's the same flask that lady had.

NANABUSH:

Yeah.

JESUS:

You stole that from her?! I didn't see you take it. When did you take it?

NANABUSH:

Hey, don't worry about it. There's crates of this where they came from.

JESUS:

Yes, but — that's theft.

NANABUSH:
Forget it. She's gone. It's still me and you 'til the tire's fixed.

JESUS:
Is that so bad?

NANABUSH:
Yes. The tire repair sets me back a few bucks. I need you to continue cutting the fifty-fifty deal.

JESUS:
Fifty-fifty for gas. Gas is all you said.

NANABUSH:
Hey. Chillax. I know what I said. But since I've been doing all the driving, come on ... how about forking in a few bucks for a new Michelin for my old Mustang. I promise, where it'll take you won't disappoint.

JESUS:
You and your bucks. You going hunting? *(he laughs.)* No. Gas was the deal. Car problem. Your problem.

NANABUSH:
(throws car keys on the bar table) You drive. Or we go nowhere.

JESUS:
I ... uh ... don't drive.

NANABUSH:
Mister Spock, you mean you don't point? It's automatic, that's all that's required these days. Point the steering wheel in the direction you're going and go! Nothing to it anymore. You don't drive! You! So smart with the memory, calculations and brilliant deductions. Mister Gitchekendawss himself. It's automatic.

You point it. That's it. This is America. Car exhaust capital of the world. You must have been … Oh man, hee hee, you're too much. Can't drink, can't chick, can't drive, can't … oh wait … this is good, tell me you're still not a —

JESUS:
Hey! Lower your voice. I like this song. It reminds me of my mother.

k.d. lang's "Diet of Strange Places" is playing on the jukebox.

NANABUSH:
Waiter! Waiter! Two drafts. You want one. Never mind, I'm going to order you one and you're going to drink it. All of it. Even if your blood boils. And this too. *(passes him the flask)* Have some. Drink to newfound friendship.

JESUS:
(listening to the song) "Internal thunder." That's her. And that thunder inside her was me. Her belly ached for me. Just below the waistline. I was the son. I am the son. The only son. Just like the solitary rising sun we see each morning.

NANABUSH:
I'm an only son too. Same. But not at birth. I had a twin. But I killed him. Well I had to. He killed our mother. He killed her 'cause he was born second. I stalked him 'til I found him. Only I could do it. She was good and she was gone. He wasn't. That's right, isn't it? To be left alone in some bush with my other siblings, a chickadee and a deer. Sisters. Grandmother. A second woman gave me life. Nokomis. Until I met the Doorkeeper's daughter. The daughter of the Western Doorway. Perhaps you'll meet.

JESUS:

    I am the son of God.

NANABUSH:

    Mnidoh so am I. Prodigal son. One of them. There's many
    more. Where's your father?

JESUS:

    Oh my father's in heaven.

NANABUSH:

    Bastard!!! Waiter ripped me off fifty cents. Helped himself to
    his tip. I was going to play a tune on the jukebox. *(just then his*
    request is played, very distinctly, The Animal's "House of the
    Rising Sun") That's the one. Animals.

JESUS:

    I was raised by a man, but he's not the one who impregnated
    my mother. My mother was a virgin. It's called immaculate
    conception.

NANABUSH:

    Immaculate conception. You! Immaculate conception?

JESUS:

    Yes.

NANABUSH:

    Some wizard dreamt you up. Conceived you in thought, then
    physicalized your likeness?

JESUS:

    Something like that — yes.

NANABUSH:
Why?

JESUS:
I'm the product of a dream, not its creator. I've struggled to understand.

NANABUSH:
G'debwe naa? You know … if truth be told, my mother was a virgin before she had me. They all were in those days. Today though, right now, changes everything. There's so much toast to be had. Waiting for the spread and butter knife. *(pause)* Did you know that fifty percent of the nutrients in fresh bread go up in smoke once you order it toasted? I don't toast mine anymore. After I heard that.

JESUS:
I wouldn't know.

NANABUSH:
No biscuit has burst for you, eh, Godfrey?

JESUS:
Uh … well … no … of course. Have you read the Bible?

NANABUSH:
No. Not lately. I've heard many good things about it though.

JESUS:
Come on. Let's go. I want to show you someplace across the road.

NANABUSH:
What is it?

JESUS:

> A house of worship.

NANABUSH:

> A church! You want me to go to church?! No way, man. You run along. I'll wait for you here.

JESUS:

> Just for a few minutes. There'll be no one in there. We'll come right back.

NANABUSH:

> You mean we'll miss the preacher. *(imitates Jimmy Swaggart)* There'll be no Lord like this Lord and I ain't no sinner.

JESUS:

> *(enticingly)* I'll put some money in for the Michelin.

NANABUSH:

> *(continues Swaggart imitation)* But if you give me your money, I'll go, for money is the only thing, besides a woman, that can move a man, amen!

Nanabush is still preaching as they rise. Godfrey is helping Nanabush who is now getting quite tipsy. They circle the stage for a journey across the street.

JESUS:

> Come on. Easy does it. Right over here. The gate to worship is right over here.

NANABUSH:

> The gate. How much to get in?

*The song playing on the jukebox fades and church organ music
takes its place. The bar table has become an altar, the beer glasses
have become chalices, a wooden cross is present and also a Bible.
A lit candle is in the center of the table, before it are others unlit.
Beside this is a small collection box. The lights dim to eeriness.*

JESUS:
> *(whispers)* See. This is me. *(holds up the cross)*

NANABUSH:
> *(looks around and whispers back)* Secret's safe with me. *(sees
> that Godfrey's very serious, he takes the cross)* Yeah?! It really
> looks like you. Pretty skimpy robe there … and how are you
> attached? What'd they do, nail you to a tree?

JESUS:
> It's cypress. A cypress cross. Real heavy.

NANABUSH:
> *(flips it over)* Made in Taiwan. So why'd you stick it out? I
> would have took off.

JESUS:
> I did. Before it happened. To here. Apparently. The other day I
> began to run. I ran in the burning sand with open sores on my
> feet. Until I became a mirage and they lost me. My followers
> lost me. They couldn't follow me 'cause they couldn't see me.
> The last thing I remember were the snarling teeth of a wild
> coyote which appeared from behind and mauled me. I woke up
> standing beside you at the pow-wow. All these years into the
> future on the other side of the world. And the first person I see
> is you? Explain that. *(pause)* You were the coyote weren't you?
> Why'd you maul me?

NANABUSH:

You startled me. Landed right on my back. My cubs nearby. How
do you expect me to react? It was my territory.

JESUS:

So you did have something to do with it. *(pause)* The crucifixion
hasn't happened yet. But it will. In a handful of years. I can't
change it. Or prevent it.

NANABUSH:

It's inevitable, right?

JESUS:

Right.

NANABUSH:

What made you run?

JESUS:

All the people wanted was miracles. More and one more.
Some weren't a pretty sight. Have you actually seen lepers?
Do you know what they look like before I cure them? The
pressure choked me. I needed breath. Politics. Church versus
state. Greed. Markets sell wares right in front of temples of
faith. That sort of thing. I believe in prayer. I mean it's not a
bad thing. To pray. Is it? You know. Give thanks.

NANABUSH:

I wouldn't want to do it in here. Too bloody quiet. And dead.
This place kind of gives me the chills. See that candle flame
— that wasn't lit before. Why are we whispering? *(he bends
to peer at a small inscription on the collection box, then reads
aloud, shattering the silence)* One dollar minimum?! This little
box is for loonies. You got to pay one dollar to light one candle.
I can get five candles for a dollar at Zeller's! I don't see any

loonies in there. I wonder who lit this one? Tell me you can at least keep the candle. I mean what good does it do being lit?

JESUS:

You light it if someone is sick or dying and you wish to send prayers to them. To get better. You can't keep it. You leave it lit. It's ... symbolic.

NANABUSH:

If there's someone sick or dying I'll go see them myself rather than run all the way over here to light a candle. Lighting a candle won't heal them. Plants can heal. Medicinal plants. Not candles. That's what heals. I mean, lighting a candle won't heal them, will it?

JESUS:

No. But the energy can make a person feel better.

NANABUSH:

It makes me feel better to watch the jingle dress dancers. That's our healing dance. And it's working. But I sure wouldn't walk up to one and try to light her wick.

JESUS:

We can all be healers. But no one wants to be. Power within. But all the faith followers need a priest or a messiah, ignoring their own channel to source and creation. We're of the Earth, the spirit world is the only place else that humans can go.

NANABUSH:

Thank you, Godfrey. That's very touching. Can we get out of here now? All this atmosphere is making you talk too much. Let's go get some fresh air.

JESUS:

Wait. I want you to read something. *(holds up the Bible)* This —

NANABUSH:

I don't think so, Godfrey.

JESUS:

Why not?

NANABUSH:

It's too big. Where would I find the time to read all this —
(takes Bible)

JESUS:

Not all of it. Just parts.

NANABUSH:

(looking at the cover) Parts about you?

JESUS:

Some —

NANABUSH:

Why not just tell me?

JESUS:

I want you to read it. Then I'll tell you my version.

NANABUSH:

I trust you. Just tell me *(gives the Bible back)* your version.

JESUS:

You wouldn't believe me.

NANABUSH:

> *(exiting)* Try me.

Jesus looks at the candle flame, then places it before him.

JESUS:

> He believes. Everything. But he does not say. Now I know.
> "Try me." Trial. Must I be tried? It's him. He is my equal. Now
> what do we do? Has he been looking for me? Prepare. Prepare
> for what? Ourselves? There's no more to prove. I am no longer
> alone. "And then said unto me, a human form in the same being
> of power and grace could serve as your brother, to teach you,
> give you word to take back." Go back? To Fatherland? Take
> him with me. Why? He would not come. Besides, he has been
> there. In ceremonies past. I love him. More than my heart. I am
> afraid no longer. Two feelings I've felt. Fear and love. Sitting
> side by side. Ready to flee. But I am whole now. Content. I
> don't want to go. I don't want to go back. To the east. I turn my
> back. I fear it over there. There is no return for me. It's all been
> a lie. Why should I go back? For torture, betrayal? Do they do
> that here? I'm confused. My confusion is making me weak.
> Mother make me stand up, straight and proud and tall like he.
> Don't send me nowhere. I won't find it. I'm gonna hide. With
> him forever. Until he sends me himself. Could that happen?
> Should it? The powers will not spare us. We will destroy each
> other. Power for power. Okay, my light, my shadow, you who
> makes my half whole. Love me like no other. Take me unto
> you. I am your faithful unless you cast me. Unless you choose
> to cast me. Bliss. Peace. Hope. Fire and ecstasy. Is it sin or
> selfishness to keep this happy soul with me from this foot
> forward. Brother. Sister. Lover. Friend. God, my father, look
> upon me now. See this smile and this tear as outer symbols of
> the rapture my whole body aches and longs for. I confess to
> you almighty one that I am happy with who I am ... as he is.
> *(pause)* But does he doubt?

Jesus is comforted by the statue of Mary suddenly glowing and very real looking.

Blackout.

SCENE 3

*Nanabush enters with the Singer carrying a
bass drum and begins to sing the American
Indian Movement (AIM) song. Brilliant lighting
changes the setting to a sunny day. The setting is
a reservation with a rustic camping site by the bay.
Jesus enters.*

JESUS:

What's that song you were singing?

NANABUSH:

That was the AIM song. American Indian Movement. Twenty
years ago my southern brothers sang that song for the first time.
It's sung in honor of our Nations. Like "O Canada." Except we
know all the words.

JESUS:

Didn't sound like words. More like a chant.

NANABUSH:

Yes, that's true. But it's its own song. You'll come to recognize its
difference from our other songs if you listen. Wanta sing along?

*Nanabush offers Jesus a drumstick. Jesus takes it and kneels beside
him before the drum.*

NANABUSH:

Okay, keep in time with me. Just beat the drum when I do.

They do.

That's it. Now sing, way ha, ha way hah ya oh heyo hey.

JESUS:

Way ha way ya weh ho ho heh.

NANABUSH:

Almost. I'll sing. You repeat. Okay? Ready? Way ha ha way
hah ya oh heyo hey.

*Another attempt is made by Jesus to sing along. On the third try
he succeeds.*

JESUS:

What does it mean?

NANABUSH:

It means *(sings)* way ha ha way hah ya oh heyo hey. *(they repeat)* Good. Don't forget to beat the drum at the same time.

JESUS:

Oh yeah.

They repeat.

NANABUSH:

Pretty good. For now you can just hum and drum. Later you'll become a singer. How about you? You got a song from your culture?

JESUS:

Ah no. Not right now.

NANABUSH:

Okay. Now I'll teach you how to dance. Okay. Like this. *(Singer beats the drum.)* Watch my footsteps. *(he dances)* Okay, you try. Let's see your footwork.

Jesus tries to dance to the beat of the drum.

NANABUSH:

Maybe we'll do it together.

Nanabush demonstrates basic footsteps. Jesus follows his lead very well. Then Nanabush starts a medium level of dance skill, slowly turning, then he goes into fifth gear with fancy footwork, spinning fast one way then the other. Jesus tries his best, then dances all wonky, out of beat. Very exhausted, he stops, falls to the ground,

catches his breath, and watches as Nanabush crescendos, then stops
right on time, hands raised, feet apart and lets out a "Hahhhh!!!"

NANABUSH:
You were doing alright there for awhile. Why'd you stop?

JESUS:
Breath.

NANABUSH:
You know I could see your steps better if you took off that
gown. You ever wear just shorts and a T-shirt? I got an extra
pair if you want.

JESUS:
(looks at his white robe) Alright.

Jesus takes his robe off as Nanabush goes to his suitcase and grabs
a pair of shorts.

NANABUSH:
(tosses the shorts to Jesus) No wonder you couldn't keep up
with all that banging and slapping going on. There's such a
thing as "Fruit-of-the-Loom" you know. *(slaps the elastic*
around his waist)

JESUS:
These are colorful. *(he struggles awkwardly to put them on)*
How do they fit?

NANABUSH:
Now you fit in. Those are the shorts I wear under my breech
cloth. Gotta flash color you know. The judge's eye must be
captured. But if I didn't know I'd mistake you for any old
American. Except for that hair on your face. *(pause)* Geez, are

you hot? Let's go for a swim. *(he gets up and stops)* You do swim? Tell me you swim.

JESUS:
Oh yes, that.

NANABUSH:
Good. We'll swim across and come back real fast.

JESUS:
You mean we'll swim all the way across the lake and back across, again?!!

NANABUSH:
Yes. Of course. What did you think we'd do — walk across?

JESUS
No, I've done that.

NANABUSH:
Well maybe we can fly.

They both transform into geese. The Singer looks up as if watching their flight. All of a sudden the winter comes and a Winter Woman enters startling the Singer who takes the drum and exits quickly.

Exeunt.

SCENE 4

*Christmas Eve. Four months later. The setting is
a bus depot. Jesus enters in cowboy attire, pissed
drunk, staggering before he falls, winding up
in one of the black and white TV chairs. Jesus
looks at the TV, reads the instructions, head
bobbing and squinting, then reaches into his
pocket for a quarter which he drops into the slot.
The TV comes on.*

TV:

Merry Christmas to all of you from the staff here at WIKY
TV5. Our next guest will be Crystal Shawanda singing, "Deck
the Halls —"

*Crystal's voice is heard singing the song on TV. Nanabush enters
wearing a black overcoat, black Levi's, and a black fedora.*

JESUS:

*(sings to the tune of Bruce Springsteen's "Merry Christmas
Baby")* Merry Christmas mister ah aha ah ah ah ah.

NANABUSH:

Mister? You talkin' to me? Merry Christmas to you too —
Godfrey!! What the heck have you been up to, I missed you
since lunchtime.

JESUS:

I've been celebrating. Birthday.

NANABUSH:

At the bus depot? Where you off to?

JESUS:

I thought I'd come here to seek destination. *(laughs uproariously)*
No, to look for you. Always find you people at the bus depot.

NANABUSH:

Keesh kwe bii nah?!! (Are you tipsy?!!)

JESUS:

That's right. Hey! Where's our whiskey flask?

NANABUSH:

That's long gone. I got smokes though. Want one? *(Jesus accepts, takes his lighter, lights up and puts the lighter in his pocket)* You smoke? I'm shocked.

JESUS:

Yes. Didn't you know? I smoke on special occasions. It's a special occasion official at midnight. Hustle bustle, hustle bustle. The last day to shop. I walk down this street and the people were just shopping and they wouldn't stop shopping. This one woman, I followed her around, bought something in every store, zoom in, look around, buy, come out, here over there, darting, she was an expert then she went and smacked her baby telling him to wait quietly for her. He wanted a ride on the plastic pony. So I gave him a quarter to pop in. That made him happy. That's all he wanted. And she was so nerve frayed by now, she looks so exhausted and utterly unhappy I wondered what all the effort was for. *(pause)* And time and time again, at almost every store — Christmas! Dollar daze!! Shop 'til you drop.

Jesus laughs, chokes on his smoke, coughs, staggers, almost falls into the lap of Nanabush.

NANABUSH:

Easy there, bud. You should sleep. Get some Z's. For the head's sake.

JESUS:

I was sleeping. In a manger. Four blocks east of here at St. Joseph's Cathedral. Huge nativity scene out front. I was sleeping quite comfortably in all that straw right beside the paper mache Jesus 'til a bunch of winos woke me up. One of them started pissing on the donkey's fur. I partied with them, right there in the nativity scene, me, three winos, three wise men, the animals, Mary, Joseph, and the baby. Of course they were all dummies.

NANABUSH:
Yes. Of course.

JESUS:
No, I mean these people don't know who I am. So I partied
with them 'til two street cops came over and gave us the boot.
Ouch! So I hightailed it over here. When's our bus leaving? We
gotta get back to the countryside. *(he looks at his watch)* Five to
twelve. I gotta do something before I leave here.

Blackout. The TV shuts off, as power goes out in the rest of the terminal.

NANABUSH:
Godfrey, I think your quarter is up. *(pause)* Godfrey?

A voice is heard in the distance, light years away.

JESUS:
I'm over here. Put a quarter in the machine.

NANABUSH:
I haven't got a quarter. Spent my last cash on this ticket and
pack of smokes. *(he hits the TV hard)* Sometimes this works.

JESUS:
Ouch! Okay, okay, Scrooge. We'll fix the wires. Big deal.

*The same black and white TV monitor appears facing the audience.
This time it's huge. Jesus' head appears in the picture.*

JESUS:
Good evening, ladies and gentlemen, children if you're
watching. I'm here to interrupt regularly scheduled
programming if I may. Allow me to have your attention.

NANABUSH:

I think you got it. Got mine.

JESUS:

Good. A long time ago in the land of Galilee, a son of a virgin woman bore a son through the magic of God. And that would be me. Witness before you Jesus Christ. I'm Jesus everyone. Today I'm 1,992. All of you viewers out there, it's my birthday. I was born in Bethlehem. A place overseas. Back east. More east than this New Found Land. I'm Joe and Mary's boy. Took for me 'til now to tell you I'm alive. 'Cause I've finally met my match. So, just to let you know. *(pauses)* Hoo boy, I feel great! And the stores will be closed tomorrow. Think about this. Anyways, my buddy's waitin for me at the bus depot so I best get on now. We will return to your *(bumbles inebriated)* progress in previously program … ah just … have a Merry Christ everybody!

Poof! The monitor goes up in smoke and Jesus stands before Nanabush. The lights in the bus depot return to normal.

JESUS:

I brought us back something. Ta dah! *(from behind his back he pulls out a half-filled 40 ouncer of Canadian Club)* Christmas party remains at that TV station. Food went all dry though. Didn't bother to touch it.

Jesus offers Nanabush the bottle. To this point Nanabush has been staring at Jesus in disbelief. He takes the bottle, downs a swig and, still staring …

NANABUSH:

Why'd you do that? You probably freaked out all the viewers. You're almost freakin' me. What has set you off? I thought you'd be okay by now. You look okay, relatively speaking, but, man, why do you always act so weird?

*Just then Kwewag enters as a beautiful young Ojibwe woman with
long black hair. She is wearing a long fur coat, mittens, and high
top boots, and walks right past them. She looks at her ticket and
the departure gate, then departs. The bus depot's Musax plays the
Eurythmics' "Love is a Stranger".*

JESUS:

Hey, baby! *(whistles)* Where you off to? Can we bus together?
Did you see that?!

NANABUSH:

Who are you talkin' to now?

JESUS:

That hot babe that just pranced by.

NANABUSH:

No one just walked by. Here, you better drink some more.

JESUS:

You saw her! She looked right at you.

NANABUSH:

Naw. Come on now. There was no one. You think I'd miss a
doll walk by? What bus did she get on?

JESUS:

She went that way. I don't know what bus.

NANABUSH:

Well, if you say so. But I've only had two gulps and I'm not
experiencing great visions like you.

JESUS:

You're serious. I think you're serious. Hey, proof's still here. Smell that perfume? Obsession. Quality scent.

NANABUSH:

That's not Obsession.

JESUS:

Yes it is. See. You smell it. That proves she was here.

NANABUSH:

It's White Diamonds.

JESUS:

How would you know?

NANABUSH:

I bought it for a certain woman for Christmas. Big fan of Elizabeth Taylor's. *(pulls perfume package out)* See. I'm going to wrap it tomorrow.

JESUS:

Really now? Let me smell. It's the same perfume. So that proves that she was just here.

NANABUSH:

It proves you wiffed this. I never saw anyone walk by, man, woman or dog.

JESUS:

You think I'm lying.

NANABUSH:

No, I think you're fantasizing.

JESUS:
> Oh sure, fantasizing about a woman that walked right past me.
> If it was my fancy I'd have her stay awhile.

NANABUSH:
> Why didn't you then?

JESUS:
> 'Cause she just walked by. Checked her ticket, checked you,
> then she left. Why would she stay? There was no time for
> conversation. Not even hello.

*Just then the same woman comes on as a bus-depot, night-shift,
minimum-wage cleaner. She is pushing a cart of mops, rags and
cleaning agents.*

NANABUSH:
> Is this your "obsession"?

JESUS:
> No. Yes. Maybe. Not ... it's not her. Before she didn't look like
> this. It is her but — er —

*He turns to search for her, then points in the direction she left,
scratches his head then approaches the janitor.*

JESUS:
> Excuse me! ... uh —

*The woman looks at him blankly and keeps on moving. Not realizing
she's been addressed, she exits.*

JESUS:
> Excuse me, miss. *(he goes after her)* Weren't you just here?

Nanabush is left on stage, laughing. The bus departure at Gate 1 is announced so he gets up and leaves.

NANABUSH
Whoa, time I better go!

Just then Jesus runs back on and finds Nanabush gone. Jesus is left alone.

JESUS:
Oh great! And he didn't tell me if he was travelling on a Greyhound or a Voyageur.

He exits after Nanabush, in pursuit.

SCENE 5

*It is winter. Kwewag enters, she is now a
Winter Woman. She swirls a blanket of snow
using white feathers. The setting is dawn on a
gravesite in a remote reserve — Wikwemikong.
A small wooden white cross stands before the
grave. Nanabush, dressed in the same blacks
as in the previous scene, kneels behind the
cross to make an offering of tobacco.*

NANABUSH:

Gchi-miigwech g'shemnido mondah giizhigut. Maaba semaa.
(Thank you Great Spirit for this day. I offer tobacco.) Everyone
suffers over the death of this little boy? What is our community
coming to? No one told me I died. I'm not dead. Jesus. Every
one talks about Jesus. Not about me. No one walks up to me
and shakes my hand to say "Bozho Nanabush." They shake
each other's hands saying, "Bozho," "Bozho," "Bozho." Each
is a part of me. Today people spend lots of money at Christmas
and the church will be packed on Christmas Eve. I'll be empty.
In the winter, houses were once full of people telling my
stories. Now they're empty just like me. They're empty 'cause
everyone is gone to midnight mass. People are forgetting the
little boy, weesehns, the child, the child in them. They don't
care about me anymore. I'm not in their hearts like Jesus is.
Jesus has replaced their mighty Nanabush. So, I keep hiding.
Hiding until I'm needed or someone calls out for me. What
good would I be to them today anyway? I am not their saviour.
Look how that burdens Jesus. He doesn't want to go back. I'm
still here. Right before your eyes. Yet you don't see me. You
won't see me, truly see me, until you're ready to give up Jesus.
I've been replaced by Jesus and yet he stands beside me like an
ally and true-life friend. He's took my place in your hearts. The
people don't say my name. Have I heard you call my name? Or
say my name since I met you … no. Fate is inevitable. I'll wait.

*Nanabush makes the Catholic sign of the cross, and recites the
blessing. He repeats it aloud in Ojibway over and over. Finally, at
"and of the son," Nanabush screams.*

That's me! That's me!!! That's Meeeee!!!!

He falls forward in anguish, knocking over the cross-shaped gravemarker. At this moment, an arrow flies upstage, from one wing, right offstage to the other wing. Nanabush feels a presence. As the next arrow is shot he turns and watches the repeated path of fire.

NANABUSH:
  When eshe mah bah? (Who's there?)

Jesus enters in full-length buckskin duds, carrying a quiver, holding his bow and reloading it. On his back he carries a huge hockey-bag knapsack, with wood and camping stuff.

NANABUSH:
  Robin Hood. Prince of Thieves.

JESUS:
  I thought I heard someone hollering their head off. I thought I missed my target. That tree stump over there. Bull's eye twice. I'm a good hunter, you know.

NANABUSH:
  I'm dead. They've killed me.

JESUS:
  You're not dead. You look quite alive. *(he moves in, puts his knapsack down)* What's that? Looks like a gravesite you're kneeling on.

NANABUSH:
  A little boy. Me in my past. This is where I was buried. A little member of our community. I missed the funeral and burial. They buried him yesterday, I guess, to put him out of the way so people could still have a Christmas to celebrate.

JESUS:

How long you been out here?

NANABUSH:

A couple hours.

JESUS:

You must be cold.

NANABUSH:

Stiffs don't get any colder than they already are.

JESUS:

Come on now. Don't talk like that. I'll light a fire. *(he unzips his knapsack for wood and matches)*

NANABUSH:

Sure. Do you know how?

JESUS:

(stops) What's buggin' you?

They look at one another. There is silence.

NANABUSH:

I'm gonna head out west. To the unknown. The place where the sun sets. Becomes black. Dark. The unknown. It's where the eighth and final fire will be lit. I want to be there for it.

Jesus clears a spot for the fire, making a small pit with the stones he's brought.

JESUS:

The final fire?

NANABUSH:

Yes. That's right. It's our Bible version. Since our world began. The Anishnaabec have lit seven fires. Each one is my grandfather. And now there is only one fire left. The Eighth. The final fire.

JESUS:

Final? Why the final?

NANABUSH:

Peace and brotherhood or destruction for all mankind. That's how the teaching goes.

JESUS:

That's it for choice?

NANABUSH:

Oh, listen for once. This is serious. You think I'd joke about this?

JESUS:

No. Of course not. It's just that —

NANABUSH:

It's just that what? *(advances towards Jesus)* You don't believe me?!

JESUS:

Hey, I believe you. Remember. I believe you.

NANABUSH:

So is that why you've come here, to bring peace and brotherhood? "Stop the wars, Godfrey is here." As you call yourself. You'll never be free of your maker. Or out on your own. You've already attracted the whole human race.

JESUS:

You can't change fate. Isn't that what you said in that southern church last summer? It's inevitable.

NANABUSH:

True. It's inevitable. The eighth fire. But even I don't know its fate. The outcome. What's in it for us? The Anishnaabec. Will we be spared because we've suffered enough because of you and your Christian Brothers. The outcome. Life or death. Eternity or darkness forever. The unknown. That's what's bugging me!

JESUS:

Are you only concerned of its effect on your people? The Anishnaabec. What about me? Us. The white race.

NANABUSH:

What about you? It's all up to you. Everything's all up to you. Materialism — imperialism. Don't you see? It always has been up to you. Everything. The fourth fire said you'd come in truth — but for greed. We knew you were coming. We were preparing to greet you. Welcome you. With open arms. But the fires have cooked. Each sputtering for oxygen. Just barely holding their flame long enough to tell us what's ahead. And the grandfathers have left us now. To fend for ourselves. They won't tell us about the eighth fire. It's up to you. Love or hate. Peace or greed. What do you want? What more do you want from us? It's up to you. Because you've been given everything. We have nothing left. You've got it all.

JESUS:

What … what can I do?

NANABUSH:

Listen. To us. The truth is the only thing we've got left. For your sake. For Christ's sake.

JESUS:

I have eight years. Then I must go back. In the year 2000. Your present future time. In my time, back home eight years from now, the people will turn on me, even my closest follower, Peter, and I'll be crucified. Nanabozho. You're not the only one who knows what's ahead. And knowing still can't prevent it. It'd upset the balance.

NANABUSH:

What did you say?

JESUS:

Balance. It'd upset the bal—

NANABUSH:

No! Before that. What did you call me?

JESUS:

Nanabozho. *(pause)* Nanabush — Waynanabozho. Those are your names people call you from different areas, right?? *(he moves to clasp his hand, Nanabush takes it)*

NANABUSH:

You … know … me. You called out to me. But my people don't.

Nanabush freezes, his back is to the audience with a side-face profile. Kwewag enters wearing the white robe worn by Jesus earlier. She is barefoot. She is smiling.

JESUS:

Yes. And I need you. Everybody does. Hello … woman.

KWEWAG:

Kwe. You want knowledge. I can give you knowledge. About the fires. My mother. The first fire.

JESUS:

> Beautiful. Pure. Woman. I've ... had ... no one. What's your
> name? *(she advances toward him, seductive)* I love you ... from
> the first time ... Kwe.

KWEWAG:

> Nini. (Man.) *(she kisses him)*

JESUS:

> Soft. So soft and fragile. I have to hold you. Tell me what you
> know. I'll listen. You're cold. You're getting cold. It's cold out
> here. On this blanket of snow. And look, you're barefoot. *(he
> lifts her up and starts to carry her offstage)* I'll be back for that
> stuff later. Will you still be here, Nanabush? Could you watch
> it? *(he doesn't wait for an answer and exits)*

NANABUSH:

> *(unfreezes)* Of course I'll still be here. I'll always be here. Just
> remember, you've only got eight years.

*He sees the Bible sticking out of Jesus' knapsack. He picks it up and
places it on top of the unlit fire.*

NANABUSH:

> Anishnaabe ndaaw. I'm no other race. And no other race can
> I be or want to be. I'm home now. I've been everywhere.
> Visiting the jungles of the world. Especially the mind. But
> it's only here. The core of the universe for me. From here
> life is meaningful. Despite the loss. I'll wait 'til someone in
> their last hour of true need calls out for me from the bottom
> of their soul. And should I hear, I'll appear. I'll continue to
> learn and pray that I'll survive this continued neglect. And I'll
> continue the disguise. *(he takes the tobacco from his pouch
> and sprinkles it on top of the unlit fire)* This is the decade
> of the Red. I come from the heartbeat of my nation. Kitche

miigwech gshemnidoh nume giizhigut. (Thank you, Great Spirit, for this beautiful day.)

Nanabush pulls a fancy silver lighter from his pocket, opens and sparks it, puts the flame almost to the unlit fire, then takes out a cigarette and lights it instead.

He re-stands the fallen gravesite cross and exits.

Blackout.

END OF PLAY

THE
TOMMY PRINCE
STORY

The Tommy Prince Story was workshopped at the Debajehmujig Theatre Group, Wikwemikong, Manitoulin Island, Ontario, in December 1994, with Larry E. Lewis and Gloria Eshkibok under a Short-Term Grant with the Canada Council awarded to the playwright.

The play was workshopped again in August 1995, with Jack Nicholsen, Sandra Laronde, Vince Manitowabi and Joey Osawabine under the direction of Larry E. Lewis from a Laidlaw Foundation Grant awarded to Debajehmujig Theatre Group. A final play workshop from the same grant award took place in October 1995, with Glen Gould, Jani Lauzon, Shandra Spears and Vincent Manitowabi under the direction of Paul Thompson.

The Tommy Prince Story was first produced at the Pontiac School, Wikwemikong, then toured to Sudbury, Thunder Bay, Kenora, Sioux Lookout, Mississauga First Nation, Wallaceburg, Walpole Island, London, Peterborough, Toronto, Kingston, Golden Lake First Nation, Ottawa, Kitigan Zibi First Nation, Constance Lake First Nation, and Sault Ste. Marie by Debajehmujig Theatre Group. The premiere was on November 11, 1995 with the following artists:

Directed by Paul Thompson
Set and Lighting Design by Stephan Droege
Costumes by Sondee Goldsack
Design Assistant – Mary Lou Manitowabi
Original Music/Composer – Jack Nicholsen with live traditional
    songs sung by Shandra Spears
Stage Manager – Jeffrey Trudeau
Assistant Stage Manager – Randy Pangowish

The cast were:
Young Tommy, Punk, Preacher,
Waiter, Traditional Dancer ....Glen Gould
Old Tommy, Tommy's Father,
Chief Peguis.......................... Kevin "Deak" Peltier
Henrietta, Father Peacock,
Tommy's Mother, Harriet, Tommy's Wife,
President Roosevelt, King George VI,
a British Lady, Mabeline, a Federal Politician,
a Drowning Woman, Beryl ....Shandra Spears

I wish to extend my deep gratitude to the following individuals:
Tommy Prince (bah) and his family, Ernest Debassige, Clarence
Pitawanakwat, Gordon Odjig, Cecil King, Lucy Odjig, Annie
Pangowish, Stanley Peltier, Lima Jacko, Paul Tedeschini, David
Duclos, Kady Jane Peltier, Violet Rivers, Papasehn Singers, all
Aboriginal and non-Aboriginal veterans, and especially Paul
Thompson, the original cast, crew and production team.

PRODUCTION NOTES

I chose to write a play about Tommy Prince because I wanted to honor his legacy and the impact of his contributions to Canada, the entire Allied Forces and to the Saulteaux people who are kin to my people — the Anishnaabec. Positive media regarding Aboriginal people is scarce, so much of my playwriting attempts to correct this.

This play originally had three actors but could easily use an additional male actor to help out on some of the roles. Originally, for instance, the Drowning Woman was actually a man but due to casting limitations we veered from historical accuracy. This additional actor could also play a female character in the Buckingham Palace scene.

Traditional songs used in the play are known throughout pow-wow country and remain popular in our community but the sound designer did compose some original soundscapes to accentuate the theater of war and other mood settings.

Tommy Prince was Saulteaux so his Aboriginal language is Anishnaabe although the dialects may vary from Manitoulin to Manitoba. In the play we utilized the local language of Wikwemikong Unceded Indian Reserve. As well, some of Tommy's lines are actual quotes from profiles on him discovered during early research for the play.

The warrior is truly a symbol of great pride in our community. Today at pow-wows it is noted that a male traditional dancer at times takes on in his dancesteps those of battle re-enactments and hunting skills for the sustenance and preservation of his family and people. In our culture an eagle feather represents the highest form of honor when given as a gift. The eagle staff is our traditional flag and enters into the circle first. Then the nation flags represented are danced into the pow-wow arena. The stage includes a riser to represent Tommy's Salvation Army room where he lives and reflects and witnesses his life story; also to the right of him is a screen to project imagery outlined in stage directions.

CAST OF CHARACTERS

Traditional Dancer
Henrietta, *a U.S. Marine*
First Responder
Old Tommy
Preacher
Young Tommy
Father Peacock
Cowgirl
Cadet Recruitment Officer
Tommy's mother
Harriet, *Tommy's sister*
Vera, *Tommy's wife*
Chief Peguis
Dispatcher
President Franklin D. Roosevelt
King George VI
Waiter
British Dame A La Edna
Dowdy Old Maid
Mabeline
Woman, at dance
Federal Politician
Major Flint
Woman, drowning
Punk
Beryl, *Tommy's daughter*

This play is dedicated to Kevin "Deak" Peltier (October 23, 1964–
October 10, 2010), a great warrior, a great Dad, and a best friend.

SCENE 1

Lights go down. A pow-wow flag song in honor of veterans begins. Henrietta, a U.S. Marine, dances in her colors led by a male Traditional Dancer carrying the eagle staff. The song ends and the warrior dancer falls dead. Henrietta runs to him, knows he's dead and picks up the eagle staff. She then rushes to the microphone at the MC stand.

HENRIETTA:

Can somebody out there help us?! Call the ambulance — he's had a heart attack! Everybody please stay calm. Move back behind the lines, the inner circle is for dancers and singers only. *(holding the eagle staff)* I'm allowed to pick this up 'cause I'm a veteran of Ipperwash. Are there any veterans out there? You know an eagle feather is the highest honor one can receive. This should be given to a veteran. Are there any veterans out there? When you make cause in the mainstream you take all your people forward, one warrior down and that's all of us down. Are you sure there are no veterans out there?

We see the flashing lights of the police and first response and hear lots of chatter. The mic is taken by a young first-response attendant. Henrietta leaves with the eagle staff. Lights down. Silence.

It's Winnipeg, 1977. A Logan Avenue Salvation Army room is recreated upstage left, on a riser to signify it is on an upper floor, about eight by ten feet with a cot and yellow spreadcover, a wooden chair and a four-drawer chest. There is a window Old Tommy looks from that is not there but implied. The upstage wall has a wooden door with a clothes hook. It is barren and cold except for the yellow blanket. Old Tommy enters from the audience.

OLD TOMMY:

Veterans — whether I'm a veteran or not, if I didn't work for a week, I don't know what I'd be doing with myself. Well I came from a poor family, I started when I was very young. I got accustomed to it and that's the way it's been going all the time. I'm still doing something. I have nothing to be sad for, I have nothing to be lonely for, I have a lot of friends. Like I said, there's always someone says, "Tom come home with me," "Tom let's go out for dinner," "Tom let's go to the bar." To me that's a pretty good life. I'm still making my money, I still have a job. I like my beer, I like my rum, I like whiskey, uh, everything, I ... I don't drink as much to turn me around and make me sick. Just drink enough. Have a good night's sleep. That's it. I work every day. I tell that to my son Tommy. Work every day and keep a good day's pay. I haven't been given a raw deal. Well I don't think so. I lived my life, I lived it the way I want. Nobody comes over and tells me what to do, nobody orders me around, so I'm living my life just the way I want to live it, that's it. I won't say I'm pleased with myself but I'm quite satisfied with myself anyway. No hangovers. No regrets.

The Salvation Army song "Count Your Blessings" plays by a marching band outside Tommy's room.

PREACHER:
(sings) Count your blessings, see what God has done. Count your blessings, count them one by one.

Old Tommy intermittently sings and then listens along. He is making his way to his room, watching a military band procession making its way to the Salvation Army chapel.

PREACHER:
Now if you were from Nova Scotia like Captain Morris and I, you would be saying, "Count your many blessings, ton by ton." Surely God gives us more than one blessing, he gives us tons of blessings. Let's continue the song only, sing *(he sings)* "Count your blessings, count them ton by ton ..."

OLD TOMMY:
(in room upstairs) I still have the dreams. I guess I never forget. I wake up in sweat and oh, it's just like being in it right over again. Nobody don't have to talk about war, or nothing. Nobody have to remind you anything, but there's times right in this very bed, right here, I wake up and just sweat. I wake myself up from yelling sometimes. To me, I think it was worth it what happened to my life.

SCENE 2

Old Tommy is in his Salvation Army room sitting on his bed. He starts to remember his first day at school when outside in the schoolyard. His teacher, Father Peacock, is on the main stage area and his younger self, Young Tommy, is kneeling before him.

FATHER PEACOCK:
Thomas George Prince. Brokenhead Indian Reserve #4. Do
you know how your reserve got that name, Thomas? *(Thomas
shakes his head)* No? Because the first inhabitants found many
skeletons ...

OLD TOMMY:
Selkirk massacre.

FATHER PEACOCK:
From the Selkirk massacre.

YOUNG TOMMY:
Selkirk massacre.

FATHER PEACOCK:
(taking Young Tommy's head and covering his ears) Wash his
face. *(he runs his fingers through Young Tommy's hair and speaks
as if to a Brother of the church or young school assistant)* His
skin can't be that dark. Let's scrub a little more. Oh — no lice.
Cut his hair. A nice trim. *(to Young Tommy)* Step forward.

*Father Peacock takes out a cloth. Young Tommy looks at the
cloth. He puts out his shoe. Father Peacock drops the cloth before
Tommy's feet.*

FATHER PEACOCK:
Clean your own shoes. *(the priest goes over to get a hoe.)* Here.
Hoe the garden with the other boys, Brother Hinton will show
you the way. You must go change into these clothes provided
for you. *(Young Tommy doesn't move; the priest goes to him
and takes his shirt off)* Pretty soon you will eat the fruits of your
labor and learn to read and write. You would like that, Thomas,
wouldn't you? *(Young Tommy stares at him)* Do you speak any
English at all, young man?

The priest dismisses Young Tommy to his orders. Young Tommy exits.

FATHER PEACOCK:
Very good, Thomas.

Father Peacock then addresses the audience as if it's the rest of the student body:

The rest of you prepare for the Grand Assembly for the first day of Elkhorn Residential School.

Lights dim on Father Peacock and a spotlight remains on Old Tommy in his Salvation Army room.

OLD TOMMY:
I liked the CPR train. I liked the way it chugged into town. Red and black. And how it whistled and when it got there it left a big puff of smoke and we got on the steel steps and took a seat. But Manitoba is boring terrain compared to what I've seen.

Young Tommy dawdles onstage, now wearing his residential school uniform and a fresh brushcut.

YOUNG TOMMY:
I make lots of friends here at Elkhorn Residential School. My number is 2418. My friend, Joseph Whippertail from Birdtail Creek Indian Reserve #57, says he's gonna leave. His house is twenty miles north of here. I told him that if he runs away, they won't ever let him back or he'll get a serious thrashing and probably won't be allowed to play hockey anymore. Joe says he doesn't care 'cause there's another residential school just on the other side of the border in Saskatchewan. I told Joe, "Why don't you climb the boxcar and jump off, Joe," but he said his brother Pete did that and broke his leg. So he can't play hockey all season. I was kicked out of kitchen duties because they caught

me taking a bite of a carrot. Everyone else had a lunch but me. But I got to go outside for our half-hour free time. That's the first time Joe had his chance to escape. We return to the books and I'm really learning math and spelling and reading. I wish there was more stories to read here. My buddy Joe likes to write his own stories but the priest told him they're not very interesting and need more depth. I'd like to punch him and put him to death. He made Joe sad for his home. He draws in his stories too. We're not going home at Christmas because our folks can't afford the 200-mile train fare. The Fathers said we could send a letter and Christmas card next week. I'll be so glad if muskrat trappings are good for my father — gosh I miss him — and Mom and the rest over Christmas. I wonder what would happen if we hopped the train home —

Footsteps are heard in sound effect.

OLD TOMMY:
Father Peacock's footsteps, I can hear them … I still can hear them.

YOUNG and OLD TOMMY:
(both kneel simultaneously) Hail Mary, full of grace … blessed is the fruit of thy womb, Jesus …

Father Peacock enters as we hear a trap snap shut. Father Peacock falls as if the trap has caught him around the ankle. He writhes in pain, but slowly transforms into a trapper's animal, a muskrat. Muskrat is now a spirit and dances as if in a ritual journey to the spirit world. Old Tommy, still kneeling in front of his bed, has taken out his pouch of tobacco and is rolling a cigarette. Some tobacco falls to the floor which becomes symbolic of a tobacco offering for taking the life of an animal, an offering that his father had taught him on his old trapline.

Young Tommy has now returned home from residential school.
Years have passed. He speaks to Old Tommy who is sitting on his
Salvation Army cot.

YOUNG TOMMY:
>   Pa, I want to be a lawyer.

OLD TOMMY:
>   Bohpa says to me, Gwiss, you just came home from Grade 8
>   and can never go back. We are Indians with a poor income.
>   What you want to be would take a lot of money. Might as well
>   not disappoint yourself. Besides, there's no such thing as an
>   Indian lawyer.

YOUNG TOMMY:
>   Well then, can I join the cadets? At least it's free.

OLD TOMMY:
>   *(speaking as Young Tommy's father)* Anninde. (Sure.)

YOUNG TOMMY:
>   I can? Yoo hoo!!! *(In Saulteaux)* Wehtaana niishin Bohpa —
>   miigwech! (Aw shucks, that's terrific. Thanks Dad.)

OLD TOMMY:
>   How the heck did I find out about cadets, anyway?

YOUNG TOMMY:
>   I seen an ad at the post office in Scanterbury one time and I
>   want to belong to something —

A Cadet Recruitment Officer enters to deliver a uniform.

YOUNG TOMMY:
>   Wow, a uniform for me! *(he puts it on)*

OLD TOMMY:

> And at once I became a better man. *(he stands before his cot to salute)*

YOUNG TOMMY:

> Attention! I place a Lee-Enfield rifle over my shoulder and I belong. Ready. I'm ready. Aim. I take it. *(he aims and shoots his target)* The Lee-Enfield rifle. Single-shot bolt-action rifle with the capacity to hold ten to twelve bullets looking at you from a magazine. I could pick off a duck from 50,000 feet away! *(he swaggers like a cowboy)* Five bullets through a target the size of a playing card at one hundred feet. They call that marksmanship and they say I've got the craft! Yes! Just wait till Friday at fourteen-hundred hours we're going to have a target game. Cinch and a half!

An old-tyme Cowgirl enters dancing to old-tyme music.

YOUNG TOMMY:

> *(pulling on a pair of worn-out cowboy boots and a gun and holster)* I'm the Texas Ranger and I know my worth. I can blow five bullets through a target the width of a cactus from one mile away. *(he pulls a gun out of the holster and spins it on his finger)* Anybody want to challenge me to a showdown? *(the music changes to "My Ding a Ling" — he returns the gun to his holster)* Well, come on there, pretty lady, let's get onto the floor. *(they dance)* I have to be a good shot. Treaty allowance is one cupful of gunpowder and three pounds of shot per family per year. So don't waste what you got! Well, we got big families, if you know what I mean. Only forty cents a muskrat skin. Trappings are not paying the tunes. But my firepower will.

Military music is heard, heralding banners that are unfurling. The banners read: Army and C.W.A.C. (Canadian Women Army Corps). There is a Canadian Recruiting Office marquee with a Union Jack hanging from it. The marquee reads: "Men, you can still volunteer, join the army to-day. Girls, you can replace a man for overseas service by enlisting in the C.W.A.C. Apply here."

We hear a drill sergeant yelling out the drills. Young Tommy learns his drills until he is perfect at it. He marches. He then steps forward in full soldier combat fatigues. He is now aboard a ship to the Second World War frontlines in Europe.

YOUNG TOMMY:

Sir, permission to speak, sir. I'm proud to join the infantry, sir. I am sailing to Europe with the 1st Corps of the Royal Canadian Engineers. Our mission is to corner the enemy then force him to retaliate. I will kill Hitler. I will stop him. With my gun. And my good shot. *(pause)* Yes I am a real live North American Indian. Thank you very much. Yes, sir. A letter, sir. Thank you, sir. *(to his comrades)* I've got a smoke signal from the Chief. Oh, it's not my dad, it's my mother who sends this —

Young Tommy has landed across the ocean. He crosses to several garbage cans, squats and sits. He then opens the letter. He begins to read. His Mother enters and speaks the letter.

MOTHER:

Dear Tommy, your sister Teresa helped me with this. I hope you are eating and sleeping, my son. I have to tell you some news that is no good. *(pause)* Your father left us. It is a good thing to be overseas. I want you to come home for the funeral Tommy but I know they will not let you. Everybody knows where you men are. I'll have all the Princes over and the Bears are cooking after the funeral service. Everyone's chipping in since we got nothing to bury him with. Uncle Andrew put up the money for the wake ... to rent the church ... give the priests something ... for his brother. I'm okay 'cause I'm so busy with the trips to town, baking bread for sandwiches, singing hymns and —

Old Tommy has been observing this life memory, perched on his Salvation Army cot. He twists an old handkerchief that once belonged to his father.

OLD TOMMY:
　　That's okay.

MOTHER:
　　The entire world knows where you are. Someday, when you
　　come home here, my son, the Canadian government will
　　welcome you and give you recognition. I will enjoy to see it
　　too, my son. All of your brothers and sisters say hello. I know
　　you are here with us. And Harriet has sent along something
　　she drew for you. I pray for you boys to be safe and come
　　home alive.

OLD TOMMY:
　　I'm alive, Mama. I wish you were alive instead of me.

Old Tommy takes out an old photo of his family from his wallet. The photo slowly appears on the screen onstage then crossfades into a drawing by a child of her pet dog named T-Bone Soup. Next we see Tommy's sister Harriet, age seven.

HARRIET:
　　Dear Brother, I'm your sister Harriet. I cut onions to put into
　　the bone soup we ate and tears start come out my eyes and
　　everyone was having fun with me I love you are brave to fight
　　in the war and be so far away. Tommy, Mommy say I got your
　　smile. Tommy, please don't cry over the onion story.

*She dances off to Hank Williams's "I'm So Lonesome I Could Cry."
Both Tommys observe her exit. Young Tommy is still by the garbage
cans; Old Tommy is in his Salvation Army room.*

YOUNG TOMMY:
(hollering like a Drill Sergeant) First assignment! Head patrol!
Protect the Allied Forces! The garbage dump! (he kicks the
garbage then returns to his normal voice) Is this all they think
I can do? I can do more than this. I'm not meant to watch the
dump. (he boxes) I need a chance, one chance and I'll prove it.
I've got to see the frontline. I just need a way. (we hear aircraft)
There's a Douglas Dakota — the Brits, C-47 — Allied. There's
a Messerschmitt 109. There is a Focke-Wulfe 190. German
missile jumper, oh, was a missile jumper, oh white doves, no,
uh, paratroopers!!! Look, there goes a Spitfire and Kittyhawk!
(splat! go the sound of seagull droppings) I joined the army to
fight, not to sit around drinking tea and getting bombed on by
seagulls. (he boxes again)

SCENE 3

The Salvation Army set has become the bedroom of Old Tommy and his wife, Vera. He's sleeping. She reads aloud Mark Twain's **Tom Sawyer** *where Tom is painting the fence and tricks his friends into taking over the job. Suddenly Old Tommy begins to moan and fidget. He is awake yet unconscious inside a vivid recurring nightmare. He bolts up from the bed to squat on the floor as if on the frontline in the war.*

OLD TOMMY:

    (in Saulteaux) Alamike. (Nazi.) Alamike. Alamike. Where's my gun, where's my gun! Where's my gun!

VERA:

    Tom, it's a dream —

OLD TOMMY:

    (locating a rifle from underneath the bed) Stop! Alamike. Alamike, the Germans are coming the Germans are coming the Germans are COMING!!!!

He points the gun at Vera, stands and backs up.

VERA:

    No! Tom! It's alright, Tom. It's just a dream, Tom. Come back to bed.

He finally becomes conscious.

OLD TOMMY:

    It happened, didn't it? Again. I won't hurt you, Vera, please don't leave me. *(he looks at his watch)* 0600 hours. Well, I'm up now, I gotta be there at seven.

He puts his robe on and heads to the interview as Vera packs her suitcase.

Blackout to a small radio studio. Tommy dresses behind a dressing screen as he does a radio interview. He speaks into the microphone standing before him.

OLD TOMMY:

    And as well as those I got the Military Medal, Silver Star, Lone Star, Croix de Guerre. What good are they to me now, you ask?

Well, I can't see no good to me at all. *(he laughs)* The army really treated me wonderful right from the start. I'd probably have still been a fisherman, or a' been digging snake root, or picking berries or something — but after I joined the army I learned something. They taught me something — how to survive. But no man can prepare another for his first drop on the frontline. There is nothing since more terrifying.

It is the Second World War. Young Tommy jumps from a plane and opens his chute. There are sounds of heavy gunfire while Tommy's beating heart is amplified. It's his first time in enemy territory. Red bullets of fire whiz past him. Tommy sweats and is terrified. Finally, he lands and runs for cover, to the trenches right on the very front-line. There are dead bodies falling all around him. Screams of killing. Knife punctures. Flesh tearing.

YOUNG TOMMY:

Comrade, please, have you got another pair of trousers? May I have them? I dirtied mine.

The gunfire is endless. There is heavy breathing all around.

YOUNG TOMMY:

Nazi pigs! Stop the tyranny! Give me more ammunition. Load this sucker. Move. Move. Move! *(in Saulteaux)* We ep we ep wenesh eh bobee tow eck! Alamike! Alamah! Gadahgwen! Gadahgwen!!! (Hurry. Hurry, what are you waiting for! Nazi! Lots of Nazis! Fire! Fire!!!)

Young Tommy engages in hand-to-hand combat with a German soldier. He becomes disarmed and lunges at his Nazi attacker. Then, from another area of the stage, we see smoke filling the space and a memorial song is heard as Chief Peguis, thirty years old (played by Old Tommy), arrives in breechcloth and red leggings with a blanket over one shoulder. There is a struggle among the three men. Peguis slits the Nazi's neck with a knife and Young Tommy mistakenly bites Peguis's nose off. Peguis reels in pain, covering his nose with a blanket. He then removes the blanket to reveal lots of blood around the wound. This area on his face is raw looking.

CHIEF PEGUIS:
That's twice my nose has been bitten. Last time from my drunk-in-love Tabush-shik! *(he smiles thinking of the woman)*

YOUNG TOMMY :
Chief Peguis!?!! You saved my life. Is that why you're here?

CHIEF PEGUIS:
That Nazi had it coming.

YOUNG TOMMY:
I'll live to have a side-arm. If I had a pistol I would have killed him. A side-arm is all I needed. *(he spits blood out of his mouth and rinses from his water canteen)*

CHIEF PEGUIS:
You fight with very awesome weaponry. I have been watching you in spirit. You are an amazing warrior. Do you know what is strange, my great-great grandson? I fled to your Manitoba to get away from the white man. And now they are all around you.

YOUNG TOMMY:
Here they are German Hitler Nazis. And they are doing the worst.

CHIEF PEGUIS:
The worst? I've dealt with foreigners for many years now. In fact, I was a foreigner myself and could not keep my people running. So we aligned with the Assiniboine against the Sioux who were allied with the Northwesters. Cuthbert Grant and William Shaw, these men, massacred the Selkirk settlers at Seven Oaks.

YOUNG TOMMY:
I don't know my enemy's names. There is only one name.

CHIEF PEGUIS:
One name they tell you.

YOUNG TOMMY:
Nazi.

CHIEF PEGUIS:
I have to know everybody's name — I am the leader. I must know where every single thing is and if not, where to find it.

YOUNG TOMMY:
Here I only hear English, or French or Italian and lots of German. It's no wonder so many orders get mixed up with all the languages we're using here.

CHIEF PEGUIS:
(he strikes his knife into the ground) This is how I deal with those who disobey my orders! No more unnecessary bloodshed.

YOUNG TOMMY:
No more unnecessary bloodshed.

CHIEF PEGUIS:
You have two options — retreat or die. Never be captured. That's a warrior. Remember too, we are not to be in battle right after the first thunderstorm. That is the time to renew your warrior soul. If you don't take that time when you go to battle your chances —

YOUNG TOMMY:
— are not so good. And that will do it.

CHIEF PEGUIS:

> And if that doesn't work I'll align myself with the church and give myself a Christian name — William King.

YOUNG TOMMY:

> Names are important.

CHIEF PEGUIS:

> And what is the son of a king called?

YOUNG TOMMY:

> Prince.

CHIEF PEGUIS:

> Aha! Then your name is Tommy Prince.

Suddenly there is a big puff of smoke. Chief Peguis screams a war cry and disappears. There is then the sound of a military bird whistle. Young Tommy arises from the trenches and packs his gear with the speed of a professional soldier.

YOUNG TOMMY:

> I'm the great-great grandson of a Chief! *(addressing a fellow soldier in the trenches)* Here, comrade, let's go into Axis lines tonight. Put on your black paint so the moon — she won't bounce off that white skin and give us away. We must find out the exact locations of enemy reserves and report all roads and bridges. Ready. Let's go.

Exeunt

SCENE 4

Young Tommy sneaks to position along the frontlines with the Allied Forces, now in the hills of Italy. He slits the throat of an unsuspecting enemy. An explosion occurs. We see an elaborate communication system with real wires coming out both sides. A cacophony of static and gunfire is heard, then silence. There is a menacing feeling of enemy eyes watching Young Tommy as he remains perfectly still in a trench.

DISPATCHER:

> (*from off-stage*) We have just lost all communication with the
> Devil's Brigade.

Old Tommy is back in his room re-living the war scene.

OLD TOMMY:

> Do you copy? Headquarters has lost us! The radio wire!
> Bombed and out.

Young Tommy knows the enemy is watching with weapons drawn.
He changes his army clothes to peasant clothing of an Italian
farmer. He then grabs a hoe and slowly begins hoeing his garden as
if working a typical day in his field. He makes his way to the frayed
wire. He momentarily locks eyes with Old Tommy.

OLD TOMMY:

> What are you looking at? We got to do something.

YOUNG TOMMY:

> (*flaying his arms in gesture as he speaks*) Fungula!! Hey, what's
> the matter for you? Look here what you done to my field where
> I growa my fresh tomatoes. Mamma mia, what do I do now?!!
> See what you do to my work. It is mine. Hey! Hey! I object!
> Where does it say you can have a war in a man's garden?!!

Young Tommy bends to tie his shoe at the spot where the
communications wire is broken. While he is bent over he fixes the
wire. Still stooped, he takes the hoe and tills the soil around him. He
straightens up, still working.

YOUNG TOMMY:

> Alla my work, my a papa's work and my great poppy's work
> and you men don't even belong here. This is Italian soil, get it,
> it's not a place for Nazis. Get out! Out!! And you Canadians

are far from home. Go back to where you came from. *(all the while he is making his way to the lookout, then ducks into it and tinkers with the radio)* Sergeant Prince, 1st Canadian Special Service Battalion, do you copy? 10-4 copy, go ahead. It's right on!!! It's right on!!! Cover me, I'm heading to re-group.

On the way Young Tommy picks up a diary from a dead Nazi's pocket and reads:

"The Black Devils are all around us every time we come into the line, and we never hear them come." Heh! You know English enough to call us your Devil's Brigade. Well, meet the devil. Shta ta ha gehn gong wah! (That's right!)

A German throws a grenade at Young Tommy and he tosses it right back.

Time shifts.

The President's March is played by a brass orchestra. First we see Old Tommy polishing his black boots; he puts them on. Old Tommy begins re-living being decorated with a medal by the President of the United States. At the same time during the following citation, we see further frontline action of Young Tommy who jumps via parachute, lands, creeps forward on his belly with the speed and agility of a snake, into a small depression to conceal himself from view. He aims his weaponry.

President Franklin D. Roosevelt sits in a wheelchair listening to his pre-recorded citation on the radio. We hear:

While in action against the enemy near Littoria, Italy, Sergeant Prince's communications were cut by shells. Using his own ingenuity, Sergeant Prince donned available civilian clothes and, under direct enemy observation, went out to his line to re-establish contact for target observation. Sergeant Prince's courage and utter disregard for personal safety were an inspiration to his fellows and a marked credit to his unit.

OLD TOMMY *is standing before his cot in his Salvation Army room. He addresses the audience:*

See, the President of the United States said it so himself. Injunuity. That's what I got. The dispatcher, who was on the other end said, "who's that out there walking around." I told him, I said "that was me, the line was cut," I said. "I went out and fixed it." And he says, "Yeah?! A bigger fool than I thought, thank you!" I just laughed. Well, I had to do something.

SCENE 5

Trumpets blow. Young Tommy stands in his London accommodation. On his chair is a new Sergeant's jacket, cap, and a side-arm gun with harness. Young Tommy quickly changes his corporal jacket and hat for these new items.

YOUNG TOMMY:

(seeing his reflection in the mirror) I earned all this. Fifty miles on foot, two battles, no food or sleep for three days. Over a thousand German soldiers were captured and many killed. I can't eat my medals but they sure make me feel good. And now I go to Buckingham Palace.

He exits to Palace almost salivating at the thought of the feast he will devour.

The Palace. Band of the Guards Brigade is played as King George VI enters.

KING GEORGE VI:

(reads the citation) In charge of a two-man reconnaissance patrol, Sergeant Prince led it deep into enemy-held territory, covering rugged, rocky mountains, to gain valuable and definite information of the enemy's outpost positions and gun locations. So accurate was the report rendered by the patrol that Sergeant Prince's regiment moved forward and occupied new heights and successfully wiped out the enemy bivouac area. The keen sense of responsibility and devotion to duty displayed by Sergeant Prince is in keeping with the highest traditions of the military service and reflects great credit upon himself and the Armed Forces of the Allied Nations.

Old Tommy has pulled his box of medals from under his bed in the Salvation Army.

OLD TOMMY:

(addressing the audience) And I could have had me the Croix de Guerre. The French Commander said, "mon Dieu!" when he realized it was just me and a private picking off all the Germans. He thought there was fifty of us. So he recommended me the Croix de Guerre. Cross of War. It's French. I would have got it if his messenger didn't go and get himself killed while delivering it. The telegraph was never received by their Commander-in-Chief, Charles de Gaulle. He's got a good name. Charles de Gaulle. So by rights, I should have me the Croix de Guerre.

Old Tommy sitting on his cot observes the medal ceremony still vivid in his memory: King George VI decorates Young Tommy with both the Military Medal and then the Silver Star with ribbon.

KING GEORGE VI:
You are Thomas George Prince?

YOUNG TOMMY:
Indeed I am.

KING GEORGE VI:
May I present to you, on behalf of the British Empire, the Military Medal for your outstanding contribution towards the Liberation of Italy. I cannot tell you how rare it is for me to be presenting two medals at once to one soldier. *(Tommy taps his side-arm)* This here on behalf of the Allied Forces, the President of the United States, President Roosevelt, has sent this Silver Star for your valor during the invasion of Southern France. Sergeant Prince, you make the Allied Forces proud to serve with you. Tell me your thoughts on service?

YOUNG TOMMY:
Your honor, your majesty, excuse me, I never really thought through this but I can tell you, I'll never again hesitate to serve with such fine comrades. Had I known what it took to serve the frontline I'd have been here sooner, not being Head Sapper to the garbage dump.

OLD TOMMY:
He looked. Then his Royal Highness, his blue-blood aristocracy, before me he stood and looked at me, me, just a soldier in the dirt and he wearing a gold-laced top hat, a scarlet red coat, blue

laced waistcoat, white buckskin breeches. I wish I was just kidding but I'm not. But the best were his black top boots and he laughed like this. *(laughs)* Almost from the belly. Only a little up here. Stuffier. *(laughs)* You know. So I said, "You met my folks on your visit to Winnipeg back in '39." *(he takes his coat from the hook, medal box in hand, and exits.)*

YOUNG TOMMY:

You met my family who arranged a gathering of the Manitoba Indian Brotherhood. They put a parade on in your honor, and your Majesty Queen Elizabeth. I had a great grandfather named after one of yours — William King. You received a pipe of peace from an elder.

KING GEORGE VI:

Oh my yes, that pipe sits on my mantle in our private quarters. It is like a sacred object to me and I cherish receiving it. Her Royal Highness, Queen Elizabeth here, wonders where other pipes can be obtained since *she* enjoys the odd puff of smoke.

Old Tommy enters; he is wearing his coat and crosses the stage to the city park.

OLD TOMMY:

"Balls! George, I do not!" "Balls," said the Queen. I heard it with two ears and a big grin besides. *(he arrives in the Winnipeg park, takes a beer from his pocket and opens it)* Here's the park now. Where's that statue again — the west side?

He stands before the statue of Chief Peguis in the park. Known as a great orator, Chief Peguis is dressed in a feathered war bonnet and a fringed, beaded tunic. The Orator has long braids studded with bits of brass.

OLD TOMMY:

See, this is the statue of the Chief I was talking about. Peguis.

That's my great-great grandfather. He took the name when he was baptized, William King. Well, uh, when his son was born, the people said, "Well, what we call him," and at that time they called him the Great One, and someone said, "Son of a Great One, is Prince," so my great grandfather took the name of Prince and was baptized Prince. To me he's a legend. Someone who could speak. And in those days, that someone who could speak and think what he wants with his people, to see better for his people, he must have had a wonderful idea.

The statue of Chief Peguis momentarily comes alive.

CHIEF PEGUIS:
   I did. I still do. It's simple. Work hard. Create results. Results mean more options. Dig, dig, dig. Retreat or die but never surrender. Don't ever give up.

OLD TOMMY:
   Well *balls*, said the Queen! Never in my whole life did I see a statue come alive before. *(he drinks his beer then salutes the Chief)* Good advice. I think I'll go to the bar.

He crosses the stage and goes to a bar counter.

WAITER:
   Excuse me sir — Indians aren't served on these premises. Management orders.

OLD TOMMY:
   Do I really have to go disguise myself and become someone I'm not just to have a glass of beer? Next time he'll be serving me. I'll just go somewhere else. After all, this is the hand that shook the hand of the King.

Old Tommy heads back to his room.

SCENE 6

*Lights come back up on Buckingham Palace.
It is a reception in celebration of all the decorated
soldiers. Military brass, Dukes, Duchesses,
other Royalty and international guests are in
attendance. The regal and proper British women
in attendance wish to talk to Tommy. And Tommy
is happy to spend an evening with all the women
present to show off his medals.*

BRITISH DAME A LA EDNA:

> *(in uppercrust British accent)* Oh my, I did not know there were Indian people who fought in the wars. I wouldn't think you would concern yourself with the war since what has all gone wrong with your country. My, my, how admirable.

She leaves in a highly affected manner. Young Tommy takes a glass of white champagne and enters the Castle Ballroom.

YOUNG TOMMY:

> Well, while I'm here I might as well enjoy this — *(in Saulteaux)* Nishkeh mampii gchitwaaa wigwam. (This entrance, this room — I'm in awe.)

DOWDY OLD MAID:

> *(in frumpy British accent)* Ahh!! Look Betty Bop, a real Red Indian — oh sir, it would be an honor for me to shake your hand. Ooo my, such strong arms. You must be a real hero to your people.

YOUNG TOMMY:

> Thank you m'am. Can't say as exactly that. But I do know why I'm here.

MABELINE:

> *(in the Southern accent of New Orleans)* Hi, I'm the Governor of Louisiana's daughter Mabeline. My father tells me you are the fiercest soldier of any man out there. A tiger is what they call you. Are you a tiger like they say?

YOUNG TOMMY:

> Where have you seen a tiger?

MABELINE:

Why at the zoo, of course. My daddy opened the State zoo.
Lady Alice Montagu-Douglas-Scott is here. She married Henry,
Duke of Gloucester, you know the one that used to sleep with
Noel Coward and is the King's brother. She'll take us on a tour
'cause she offered it to me before. When I go home I'm gonna
ask my daddy to build me a castle — just similar to this one!

YOUNG TOMMY:

Don't hold your breath on that one.

*Mabeline flirts with Tommy. He shifts his shirt collar as he begins
to sweat.*

MABELINE:

Oh you upsters — come on — I'll show you where King Henry
VIII kept all of those wives.

YOUNG TOMMY:

(hesitantly) Sure … *(they exit)*

*Old Tommy is back in his room sitting on his cot, reminiscing about
that incredible evening of honor.*

OLD TOMMY:

I wanted to go with that girl but I didn't want to miss my ride.

*Military music comes on. Young Tommy re-appears on a military
supply ship.*

YOUNG TOMMY:

The Nazis have surrendered. We're sailing back to Canada. I'm
going home. Look at those waves, look at that deep water. Five
years. Can you believe it! Europe, you're one helluva place. I'm
finally going home!

OLD TOMMY:

>   No more war. I didn't know anything but war.

YOUNG TOMMY:

>   See way out there? That land approaching? That must have
>   been what Champlain saw.

*Young Tommy is now back on land in Canada. He crosses the stage
to a radio studio microphone for an interview.*

YOUNG TOMMY:

>   Well, I'm happy to be back here and that the war is over. *(he
>   is nervous and knocks the mic down)* Heh. First time on radio.
>   Better than the boat ride. Canadians should be proud of the
>   hard work of every Canadian soldier and that includes all of us.
>   When you honor me you honor all of us. We needed each other
>   to make a strong front and believe me, we often saw the front
>   without bullets left in our rifles. We covered each other to get
>   more ammo real quick. I return to civilian life. On my Indian
>   reservation in Brokenhead.

*It's five years later in Brokenhead. Young Tommy smashes an axe
to chop a block of wood in two. He stops to take a break. He swigs
from an army flask. Flies are buzzing about, birds are singing.*

YOUNG TOMMY:

>   Mama, I can't stand it here anymore. I've gotta get out of here.
>   I look out at these balsam trees and cut them. I take my axe and
>   sell the wood. I sell it and sell it and sell it and I'm not getting
>   anywhere. I need the city. I need action.

OLD TOMMY:

>   *(from his Salvation Army room)* When there is no sun in
>   Brokenhead it is so bleak.

YOUNG TOMMY:

> And the highway just barrels right between here. *(a transport zooms by)* Hey, slow down — kids live here don't you know! *(tires brake)* Great for the Bear's store business — but we live on top of muskeg.

OLD TOMMY:

> They let me serve with total freedom then shipped me back there to be a prisoner?!

YOUNG TOMMY:

> See — muskeg. It is just like them to stake this reserve on this type of soil where no vegetables can grow. *(he pulls on his cowboy boots)* Well, there is always the Saturday night party!

The song, "Frankie and Johnny" plays. It's 1945. Young Tommy is in a dance hall. A woman enters and tries to get Tommy to dance, he rejects her advances, she leaves and then returns. She has a broken beer bottle.

WOMAN:

> You think *you're* better than us, eh?! — 'cause you went overseas? — you're not!

YOUNG TOMMY:

> Hey, I didn't come home to fight!

She goes to Tommy and attacks him with the beer bottle, cutting his cheek from the bottle's broken edge. He puts his hand to his cheek to stop the blood flow and they lock eyes in horror. He runs home and sews his own stitches. He's a warrior, he's tough — he doesn't go to the hospital over an hour's drive away nor does he fight a woman.

YOUNG TOMMY:

> Squekedyahtkamikbehmdahgeshshugwah!!! *(swears in Saulteaux, swigs his whiskey, tears swell)* No more. No … *(he gasps in pain)*

... if I don't leave this place I'm going to die. Who's there — I can feel you — who is it? *(Harriet is in a full-length flannel nightgown. She creeps around the corner)* Harriet ... Harriet, what are you doing? You should be asleep.

HARRIET:
What happened, Tommy?

YOUNG TOMMY:
I just ran into a little bad luck tonight. But, little sister, I know what to do now.

HARRIET:
Tommy, you look sore.

YOUNG TOMMY:
I'm okay. Nmaaja nishiime! (Go little sis!) Go to bed before somebody else gets up.

HARRIET:
Bye, Tommy. I won't be seeing you in the morning, will I?

She exits.

A road scene outside on the reserve. A car goes by. Tommy sticks out his thumb. The sun rises.

Black and white footage of Winnipeg is projected — a big bustling city in the late 1940s. Young Tommy, wearing a janitor's jumpsuit, is invigorated by his new lifestyle.

YOUNG TOMMY:
(scrubbing floor with a mop) Okay, I'm fully stocked of cleaning supplies for one month. There's a new restaurant opening around the corner — I'll land that cleaning contract

first thing in the morning. If Vera has a boy it's going to be Tommy Jr. If it's a girl we're going to call her Beryl! *(the telephone rings)* Prince Maintenance. Princetenance. Hey really! I'll be right there. *(he hangs up, grabs his jacket)* She's going in, she's ready to go in, oh boy — oh girl! Oh yes!!

Young Tommy runs out.

Old Tommy goes to his jacket hanging from a coatrack near the door, digs out a letter envelope and opens it. This is the same setting where the nightmare scene occurred earlier in the play: the Salvation Army room cot doubled as his Winnipeg home shared with his wife Vera.

OLD TOMMY:
   (he reads the letter) We the Manitoba Indian Brotherhood need a strong spokesman, and all of the voting chiefs have unanimously chosen you to be our chairman and to negotiate, on our behalf, and represent the province's Indian population before government.

Young Tommy returns to a spotlight at an opposite but equal balance on the stage as if the two Tommys have become one person. This punctuates the importance of this moment in his life — that of being needed as a leader.

YOUNG and OLD TOMMY:
   I could do that!

Young Tommy has put together speech notes for his conference with government officials. He looks them over as lights dim as if before a podium. Old Tommy turns and is instantly back in his Winnipeg house setting.

OLD TOMMY:
   Vera, did you hear that? *(we hear the water taps filling a bath)* What an extraordinary offer. Okay, first I'll need some help.

Buzzigim (My dear), listen to this alright, June 5th is coming quick. I have to table a brief to the Commission to make changes to the Indian Act. I'm going to start writing. What do you think I should include?

VERA:
First get their trust. Explain to them that everything you say is true because you live inside the life of being an Indian.

OLD TOMMY:
Yes, reserve versus city. Urban. Rural. Government must realize what the city can do for us in terms of jobs.

VERA:
Of course they do know there are few jobs on the reserves by now, other than at the school or band office, pretty much. Government put us on the reserves. The law says the only way to live off reserve is to enfranchise. Sell your status rights to the Indian Agent. But I want to be able to live on-reserve there too, you know, to get away from them once in awhile. Perhaps we should ask for things on behalf of those back home only.

Old Tommy crosses to the point on-stage that balances him with Young Tommy to set-up this speech to the government committee. It is spoken by both Old and Young Tommy, but delivered as if by one man.

OLD TOMMY:
Good morning, gentlemen. My name is Tom Prince. Brokenhead Indian Reserve and member of the Devil's Brigade.

YOUNG TOMMY:
I have prepared this brief which is very straightforward. It outlines what our basic issues are and I would like to begin with a summary.

OLD TOMMY:

I was appointed to this post by my people. My life on the reserve was as a hunter, trapper, and woodsman. In service I was an army patrol leader. Three thousand Indians served in the army during the Second War.

YOUNG TOMMY:

These men broadened their knowledge and fought with the Allied Forces to bring down the tyranny of Hitler and were successful. Many, including myself, have been decorated for service duties.

OLD TOMMY:

In turn for this, Canada should recognize us, and every Indian war veteran should be given the opportunity to provide leadership among their fellow Indians. The people living on the reserve need money to start businesses and farms which could get all of our Indian band members working. On the reserve, we are still catching up to what I see and hear in the city, and with the rest of society.

YOUNG TOMMY:

Our special rights to fish, hunt and trap must be protected until the transition to a modern lifestyle has been made. I myself operate a successful cleaning business in the city of Winnipeg, which I started, to feed my family.

OLD TOMMY:

It is not an easy thing to walk around these streets wearing this dark skin and being made to feel like I should go back to where I came from. I sold my Indian rights in order to work. To leave the reserve. To get a blue card to go to the Legion. Any number of reasons are useful.

YOUNG TOMMY:
> We look ahead as people. It's not going to be easy or happen
> quickly. But it's exactly what we need.

FEDERAL POLITICIAN:
> Sergeant Prince, sir. Fundamentally, your requests are clear.
> However, I must point out that it seems that assimilation is
> working for you. Why can it not for the rest of your people?
> You have done what you have done. What can government do
> to move others of your kind?

OLD TOMMY:
> I fought in service for five years and saw lots of places. I like to
> work. It works for me. And now I'm in this role for change for
> all of us.

FEDERAL POLITICIAN:
> Task demands can be looked into — although one could project
> that any relationship between government and Indians shall allow
> for advice and intervention on a continual basis. It is a touchy
> subject matter so solutions aren't easy since we know the benefits
> of integration and the costs of the reserve system — but heavens
> by no means shall we ignore the contribution of Canadian soldiers
> who fight our wars, lest we forget — *(he strikes his heart)*

OLD TOMMY:
> Lest we forget the frontline contribution of many Saulteaux
> Manitoba brothers.

FEDERAL POLITICIAN:
> Yes, them too. I promise that government will make sure that
> the Manitoba Indian Brotherhood be recognized for its strength
> and lobby efforts. These committee hearings are so useful.
> We're re-structuring. You're aware of the Indian Act's hearing
> budget, and Manitoba's small portion?

OLD TOMMY:

Well let me go to Ottawa. Or let me see the King, I've talked to him before.

FEDERAL POLITICIAN:

Government does not see the need for an Indian to vote Tommy, since you are considered wards of the Crown. Indians are special cases, Mr. Prince. You are a soldier, Tommy, you enfranchise and you can vote. Mr. Prince, you are going to be a Canadian citizen. But the remainder of your people, Tommy, shall remain wards of the Crown and shall be taken care of. Their contribution shall never amount to any significance in the progress of this country. War or no war, Sergeant!

YOUNG TOMMY:

Well thank you just the same for absolutely nothing but words. My people have given me a mountain and you have given me a pick-axe. I cannot move a mountain with just a pick-axe.

OLD TOMMY:

You make me wonder why I fought for this country in the first place. You do not even take care of your own. My people starve for one meal a day. Some horrifying scenes occur on the reserve more horrifying than the Nazi destruction I saw in Italy.

YOUNG TOMMY:

I appeal to your sensitivities here, sir. However, I see you have none. I resign from the Manitoba Indian Brotherhood. I pass the hat to another of our people. The status you leave us people — the true keepers of this country — wears me down. I cannot live with this responsibility anymore.

FEDERAL POLITICIAN:

Whatever you say, sir.

The stage lighting shifts which ends the committee hearing.

We hear truck tires screech and smashing of glass. A bottle of cleaning soap tips over. Old Tommy lifts it up. Young Tommy crosses the stage beside him. Both Tommys are reliving the employee betrayal that sank Tommy's cleaning business. The shamed employee is nowhere to be seen as if he's running from the scene of the crash.

OLD TOMMY:
   My truck!! My business.

YOUNG TOMMY:
   (to off-stage employee) How could you do this? — you just started two weeks ago and look what you've done. You're drunk! *(to Old Tommy)* Taking my company vehicle without consent. If I don't get insurance, I'm history and so is my business.

Young Tommy is menacingly close to Old Tommy for a frozen moment.

OLD TOMMY:
   Well at least he didn't bite off my nose!

New army music is playing. It is 1950 and Prince has re-enlisted in the Korean War. Herald and banners are used to wave away the boats to war. Young Tommy is aboard one. Old Tommy has retreated back to his Salvation Army room upstage.

OLD TOMMY:
   We shall go to the 38th parallel! Every decade has something in it. In 1940 I joined the Second World War and now I'm heading for my second service: 1950. This time Korea!

YOUNG TOMMY *(now a Drill Sergeant)*:
   Sir, permission to speak, sir — that comes from me, Sergeant

Prince — Line! Attention! You're in the Princess Patricia's now.
You are hard! You drink hard! You play hard! You love hard!
You hate hard! You fight hard! You can decide what you drink,
how you play, who you love. We'll decide who you hate and
who you fight! Remember that and you may live to boast of
your war exploits to your kids.

Time shifts from the training session to Young Tommy's officer's tent.

YOUNG TOMMY:
Soon I was in Korea but no more Devil's Brigade. This time the
27th Commonwealth Brigade. Different war but frontline action
never changes.

Old Tommy sits on his cot. We hear a 49er pow-wow song being sung.

OLD TOMMY:
General MacArthur said the only way to judge a fight is to see it
yourself. I was a Sergeant in charge of training for the Princess
Patricia Canadian Light Infantry. May I tell you a story about
war. And the 49er songs. Fifty Indian men fought in one unit of
127 men. A few men of the fifty would sing songs around a drum
that they made out of burlap when they got there. They sang them
at night to their loved ones, to pass the time, the waiting, when
there was no one within a fifty-mile radius around, they'd sing
(he joins the singing) "If you'll be my sugar honey, I will be your
sweetie pie, he yah ha he yah ha yoh." I liked them singing, we
would laugh and visit and have French wine. Maybe that's the
time that would make your eyes wet, laughing, keeping alive,
and remembering and wanting to see your family. We lost only
one Indian man, then there were forty-nine. And you know, there
were only forty-nine white men too. We fought together, leading
them, making the most out of reconnaissance maneuvers, that's
when you lose them, this is a dangerous service. Death is more
immediate than life. But you can't let yourself fail. But you're not

thinking of dying for your country — you're thinking of staying
alive and protecting your ass.

*Two consecutive combat scenes of frontline action in Korea are staged.
Routine 1 is choreographed and performed by Young Tommy and an
actor in Korean fatigues emphasizing battle danger and the enemy:*

*Cold winds, drenching rain, war with the North Korean troop.
Small-arms fire. Forced to crawl on hands, knees and bellies to
reach enemy lines. Enemy flees.*

*Young Tommy then quickly dresses for Routine 2 where he is a
comrade with other U.N. troops:*

*Snatch Patrol briefing drawn into sand, a small flashlight illuminates
the plan: cross No-Man's Land separating the United armies from
those of North Korea. Infiltrate enemy positions during the night,
quietly and quickly locate a lightly guarded machine gun. Kill the
soldiers, dismantle the gun, and return with it to the U.N. line.
Tommy briefs the strategy as his comrade applies black paint to his
face: no talking; sign language only.*

OLD TOMMY:
Indians are the right color for Snatch Patrols.

*Blackout. Drums accentuate the dark. No-Man's Land is pitch
black. Young Tommy crawls on hands, knees and belly; it is black-
light. He stops. He squeezes the man's hand behind him. He motions
for everyone behind him to stop. He strikes a match. He points to
the wire. He takes out toilet paper and wraps it around the wire in
his path. He squeezes the hand again and moves on. Two machine
guns are discovered by Prince, who has crept to the unsuspecting
enemy. He kills four soldiers with knives, strips the two machine
guns from their tripods and heads home as dawn breaks. We hear an
aircraft fly by overhead.*

MAJOR FLINT:

Tom, you take too many chances and threaten the men under your command with their lives. And your physical condition seems waning —

YOUNG TOMMY:

Ha! I'll take on any member of my platoon and we'll have an endurance competition and then the winner can take on your troops. Game!

OLD TOMMY:

And what do you expect, tempers to never flare?

YOUNG TOMMY:

Americans fired on the Patricias — an accident — you got the wrong men! Men withdraw immediately. Stop. Attack.

MAJOR FLINT

(on radio) Sergeant Prince!

YOUNG TOMMY

(on radio) Yes, sir.

MAJOR FLINT

(on radio) The Chinese are gaining a foothold on the forward positions of a U.N. unit. We must assist to recapture the post. Copy.

Tommy attempts to recapture the post but is gunned down and shot in the knee.

MAJOR FLINT

(on radio) Status report. Status report! All units. Copy-copy-copy! Five Patricias were killed on the Hook and nine were wounded, one was Sergeant Prince. Sergeant Prince, you are discharged honorably from active service.

YOUNG TOMMY:
>   *(on radio)* No! I want to fight! *(to himself)* Balls — arthritic knees.

MAJOR FLINT:
>   *(on radio)* We are sending men to get you. Copy! You stay in hospital, recuperate, see what we can do for you, there are many men, don't feel obligated to serve, you are dispensable. 10-4. Over and out.

YOUNG TOMMY
>   *(on radio)* But I belong in service, sir. It is all I know, sir. I go back home and I got nothing, sir. Absolutely nothing, sir. Is all I'll be is an Indian sir, with no vote, no right to leave the reserve or enter the bar or Legion. I was told I would get these things if I enfranchised, sir, but it didn't happen yet, sir. Here I am treated good, sir, with respect, sir — *(he puts an unconscious soldier on his back)* — please grant me permission to stay, sir, at home I am just an Indian. Sir? Copy, sir? I Sergeant Prince order you to copy, sir —

Silence.

We see Young Tommy wobble to his feet and exit the frontline with the fallen comrade on his back. The emotional loss of no longer being in active service is monumental and supported by a soundscore that captures Tommy's state.

Blackout.

SCENE 7

It begins to rain. Lights up on Old Tommy wearing a tattered overcoat with a whiskey bottle in his hand and an empty paper bag on the ground. He's on a downtown Winnipeg park bench — the same park that has the Chief Peguis statue which is projected on screen. It's 1965.

OLD TOMMY:

Well, at least I've got this whiskey bottle and my park bench.
Yess sirreee! And the street patrol say "Goodday Tommy, Sir."
They know their veterans. And once a marching band went by,
a young drill sergeant shouted to me "Sir" and saluted me until
I stood up and saluted him right back ... and everybody ... and
had I been born a white man I could be someone today. Nobody
could take me down and not a moment I can let outside of my
head, or inside my body ... shrapnel ... my entire spine ... filled
with shell fragments ... it keeps tickling my bones, four straight
good ones. As soon as I put on my uniform I felt a better man.
*(he puts the empty mickey back in the paper bag and tosses it in
the trash)* Would it look bad? To praise an Indian, to admit, to
realize we're not afraid of you. Well, I ain't gonna carry no gun
around with me, but I got these two hands.

*We hear a woman screaming for help and water splashing. Enter
Young Tommy who races to the edge of the dock, lies on his stomach
and reaches for the drowning woman. She is in a state of shock and
begins to pull Young Tommy towards her so he puts a stranglehold
on her, and lifts her onto the dock and resuscitates her.*

WOMAN:

(sighs and sobs) You saved my life, I fell, I, I lost balance, the
current took me, I don't know how to swim — my children —
please let me pay you?

YOUNG TOMMY:

Oh, it was nothing really, as long as you're okay, you might
be in shock for awhile. I heard someone scream and all these
people are just standing around watching you so I knew what to
do, I been there before —

WOMAN:

Your courage is amazing, what's your name?

YOUNG TOMMY:
Tommy. Tommy Prince.

WOMAN:
Thank you, Tommy Prince.

A large newspaper is projected showing front-page coverage of local hero, Tommy Prince.

OLD TOMMY:
I kept that clipping, with all my citations, and letters overseas, and pictures, but they were all destroyed in the apartment fire I was in last week. You can't do anything about fire damage except just start over. Like that drowning woman heading home to her children with a renewed outlook. I want another chance. Especially with my baby daughter — Beryl. I wonder how she is? Maybe she saw that newspaper and knows I'm still around. I imagine she's a great reader and will write me someday. I like coming here to see Chief Peguis's statue and soon can you believe they will be making one of me!

SCENE 8

*It is dark in inner Winnipeg. A city punk runs
in and lunges towards Old Tommy.*

PUNK:

Hey mister — give me everything you got or I'll slash your throat.

OLD TOMMY:

Oh yeah. I got thirteen dollars in my right pocket. That's all I got.

As the punk reaches into his pocket, Old Tommy begins to fight him off.

PUNK:

Hey, come on, old man!

OLD TOMMY:

I'm not your old man.

PUNK:

You're older than me I can tell.

OLD TOMMY:

Must you rob people?

PUNK:

It's called survival.

OLD TOMMY:

War is survival.

PUNK:

Living here is war.

They struggle, the Punk brandishes a switchblade and slashes at Tommy's ear. Tommy releases him and backs up.

OLD TOMMY:

You kill for money?!

PUNK:
> You'd do the same.

OLD TOMMY:
> I earned eleven war medals.

PUNK:
> Get out of here, old man. Go home.

*The Punk has put a gash in Tommy's ear with the knife and runs
off counting the bills. Old Tommy is bleeding. He covers up the
ear with his hand as he shuffles along the sidewalk heading to the
Salvation Army where he goes to his room.*

ANNOUNCER:
> *(on the radio)* And here is Buffy-Sainte Marie to sing
> "Universal Soldier." *(the song plays)*

OLD TOMMY:
> *(as he bandages up)* I wouldn't fight for the punks of this city,
> but I'd fight for the people of my generation any time. What's
> that voice? Those words make sense to me. Who is this Buffy
> Sainte-Marie? I give all of my children to Children's Aid
> thinking I would help them. Now I don't know where they are
> or how they're doing. I might not ever see a comrade again
> but I want my baby back! And so you know what I did — I
> realized something about myself — my drinking is getting to
> me — I can't control myself sometimes — I have to kill the
> pain, especially my knees. All that paratrooping and climbing,
> and walking for days in a row on them. The Salvation Army is
> available and that's where I'll go even if it means — *(he sings)*
> "Count your blessings, see what God has done." *(now talking)*
> Every day, one day at a time — I must see Beryl. I wonder if
> she still knows me — or would care to.

Time passes. Old Tommy lies down on his cot. The medal box slips off the bed — it is empty. A young woman, Beryl, Tommy's daughter, has arrived on the street in search of her father.

BERYL:

> Have you seen Tom Prince? At the National — uh, excuse me, mister. Have you seen Tom Prince?

WAITER:

> Hey, you coming to take him home. He's one helluva lucky man. He's got a room at the Sally Ann — third floor — that's his window.

BERYL:

> Thank you, thanks a lot!

Beryl races to find his room. There is a knock at the door of Tommy's Salvation Army room. Old Tommy goes to the door. It's Beryl.

BERYL:

> Hi. Daddy. It's me, Beryl.

OLD TOMMY:

> Beryl, my Beryl. Come here — Beryl, my baby. Where shall we go? — I'll take you to dinner — did you eat dinner?

BERYL:

> Yes, but I'll come along.

OLD TOMMY:

> Oh Beryl, today something good happened.

BERYL:

> Dad, why don't you come to my apartment and I'll cook you a dinner and I'll invite the whole family over?

OLD TOMMY:
Beryl — I have missed you — how did you find me?

BERYL:
Well first I went to the National Hotel and then I waited next door at the coffee shop hoping you'd walk by. And then a waiter told me I'd find you here so I came right over. Dad, I had to find you — we all miss you and everybody loves you. Come on Dad, I'm gonna take you home.

Young Tommy enters and is in Brokenhead. He is considerably older, walks with a slight limp. Old Tommy crosses to his cot in the Salvation Army one last time.

YOUNG TOMMY:
(on the river bridge on the Brokenhead Reserve) And now I'm going to be featured in a documentary film. Imagine! So the first place the producer wants to go is here. Brokenhead Reserve. Forty minutes north of Winnipeg. Why do they always bring me out here? So I can start from the beginning. You know I've been interviewed before — how come I have to start over every time? Don't you people keep those papers? *(pause)* I'm used to Winnipeg. You see, I left this reserve quite some years ago, I spent time in the army, I been over on the other side for quite some time and I came back here. I tried it for a year and a half and I couldn't stand it any longer. Nothing against the people. Well, I'm used to city life. No action. Too quiet. Too quiet. No, I don't ever think I will go back. I have my ... The only time I'll come back here is feet first.

SCENE 9

Headlines about a Pauper's grave unfurl. A casket is elevated with a Canadian Flag. The screen footage is that of a black and white funeral procession from 1977. "Battle Hymn of the Republic" plays. The live procession includes Beryl sobbing. The bugler plays the "Last Post." Lights come up on Old Tommy sitting on his cot.

OLD TOMMY:

> Memories. Especially when they blow a Tap. The "Last Post."
> Makes you think you're going through it. We lost a lot of men,
> no doubt about it, there's no use saying, no use hiding behind
> the bush, we did lose a lot of men. Now a lot of them walking
> around with just one leg, a lot of them walking around with
> just one arm. Then you start thinking about these things, and
> the way that "Taps," and everybody's silent, is uh, a thousand,
> a million pictures goes right through your mind, in your own
> mind, right there.

*We take the audience back to the Opening Scene with Henrietta, the
U.S. Marine. The "Flag Song" begins, she dances into the pow-wow
circle carrying the eagle staff.*

HENRIETTA:

> You know I've been trying to find a veteran to give this to and
> now I've found a keeper for this eagle staff — Tommy Prince.
> I want to start a Tommy Prince Scholarship Fund. His children
> will be guardians of the five eagle feathers on this warrior staff,
> each is for one of them. Gchi-miigwech, you make me proud to
> know such a "good" soldier.

*She salutes him then sings an honor song. The male Traditional
Dancer re-enters and is now a spirit dancer.*

TRADITIONAL DANCER:

> There. That's the story of Tommy Prince.

*Lights come down on the main stage leaving a solo spot on the
empty cot of Old Tommy. Light fades to black.*

Blackout.

END OF PLAY

BORN BUFFALO

Born Buffalo was workshopped by Askiy Productions thanks to the support of the Saskatchewan Arts Board and the Canada Council for the Arts.

Askiy Productions was co-founded by Kennetch Charlette and Alanis King as Co-Artistic Directors from 2009–2011. *Born Buffalo* was Askiy Productions, mainstage project the collective created, developed, produced and toured provincially in 2011.

Born Buffalo was a workshop production in conjunction with Wanuskewin Heritage Interpretive Centre, Saskatoon, Saskatchewan in 2010. In July 2011, the world premiere and provincial park tour kicked off at Saskatoon Friendship Park, Prince Albert National Park, LaRonge, Meadow Lake Provincial Park, Buffalo Pound Provincial Park, Saskatchewan Landing Provincial Park, and Echo Valley Provincial Park with the following:

Directed by Kennetch Charlette (2010) and Alanis King (2011)
Choreography by Jackie Latendresse
Set Design by Adrian Stimson
Costume Design by Jeff Chief
Design assistance by Trina Carter, Nicky Geraty, Sadie Nydigger, and Danielle Roy
Sound Design by Kristin Friday
Stage Manager, Joey Rump

The cast were:

Lucie . . . . Brenda Animikwan
Jesse . . . . .Lanny Macdonald
Dr. Palen . . . . .Mitchell Poundmaker
Zookeeper . . . . .Lacey Eninew
Meshe . . . . Gloria May Eshkibok (2010)
. . . . .Jennifer Dawn Bishop (2011)
Rusty/White Buffalo Calf . . . . .Lacey Eninew

The author wishes to thank Debra Ness, John Lagimodiere, Cecil King, Catherine Littlejohn, Tribe, Lori Blondeau, Hugh Tait, Lorne Gardipy, Adrian Stimson, Wes Fineday, Margaret Pitawanakwat, Wanuskewin Centre, and the entire production team and tour hosts. Special thanks to Elizabeth Bitsy Bateman and to Jackie Latendresse of Free Flow Dance who helped shape the play through exploration of buffalo movement and choreography.

PRODUCTION NOTES

This one-act play is an homage to the buffalo cultures of the prairies and was therefore performed outdoors. A large stuffed buffalo was masked in design to look like a butte. Painted backdrops resembled the prairie and the river. In casting *Born Buffalo*, the choreography is integral to the production as the movement of the buffalo lends the play its magic and humor. Created in Saskatchewan, I chose to utilize the Cree language in addition to my own Odawa language.

CAST OF CHARACTERS

Lucie
Jesse, Lucie's twin
Dr. Palen
Zookeeper
Meshe, a buffalo
Rusty, also White Buffalo Calf

Kina n'dahwendahgnug gye kina mashkode-bizhikewag.

*Two Grade 10 high school students are tourists
entering at an outdoor amphitheater near the
entrance of the city zoo. The theater is carved
right into the bedrock sloping down to the
spacious stage area. There are trees and grassy
areas behind the stage; the amphitheater's
backdrop lends to the setting of a buffalo's
natural landscape. It is a cloudy day and zoo
animals can be heard in nearby cages. The
students are fraternal twins Jesse and Lucie,
who carries a large picnic basket. They make
their way to the front row seats talking in hushed
tones typical of teenagers looking for a seat in a
theater: "Nobody ever sits in the front anymore,"
"Just sit down — they're about to start."*

*A scientist, Dr. Palen, enters and begins his
lecture center stage.*

DR. PALEN:

> Thank you for bringing me here. I'm Dr. Palen the Third,
> an American. I know. Three generations of genealogists
> specializing in genetics — figure it out, why that's enough
> knowledge to make a species survive. Were it to be human. I
> switched my major to the bison.

*Dr. Palen recreates a couple buffalo moves trying to lure the
young students into his lecture; he has flashes of buffalo movement
brilliance but he is stiff and awkward. He then raises his nose on
which his eyeglasses sit and looks up and down at the assembly,
takes a breath and frowns.*

LUCIE:

> This is boring.

JESSE:

> Yeah, let's take off to the back of the zoo section — *(pointing)*
> there. No one will miss us.

LUCIE:

> Alright!

They sneak out quickly, ducking their heads, hoping not to be caught.

DR. PALEN:

> *(continuing lecture)* I really tried to study the alligator like
> my forebears but the swamps — I couldn't hack the south!
> Switched to bison — just as unpredictable, just as dangerous.
> And now I get to travel to Canada! Y'all got bison sanctuaries
> to visit. Plus, some places where your bison went extinct
> the natural landscapes are still intact for paleontological
> exploration. Much like *arr* American Great Plains interior.

His Zookeeper assistant enters holding up a replica sample of an ancient bison.

DR. PALEN
    (checking out Zookeeper) What are you doing after work? Wanta talk fossil reproduction?!

ZOOKEEPER:
    (blankly) Sure.

DR. PALEN
    Really?!

She dumps the bison replica in Dr. Palen's arms and exits.

DR. PALEN:
    See this? This specimen here is thirty six thousand years old. Blue Babe, a dead buffalo bull. American lions got him. Y'all know how I know that? Matches exactly with a lion's jaw replica of this era. Mind boggling, eh?!

Zookeeper re-enters with a bucket of water and pretends to throw it at Dr. Palen, but at the last second pours the water in a trough in a nearby fenced cage.

DR. PALEN:
    Lions in America thirty six thousand years ago. See, these tooth and claw marks fit perfect! Frozen right into his hide. And this color — it's copper precipitation. That's what gives it this blue tint. Blue Babe. Probably under a year old at the time.

Almost in tears Dr. Palen gives the prop over to the Zookeeper.

DR. PALEN:
    So are we still on for later?

ZOOKEEPER:
   (under her breath) Fossil.

DR. PALEN:
   I'm here to share the scientific history of the bison, the
   phylogenetic steps. Think of a pastry, a croissant, how it's made
   of phyllo dough, the layers it represents. Delicious!

*Dr. Palen freezes. Lights come up on Meshe, a female bison, who
stands inside a white picket fence which marks her cramped living
quarters in the zoo. Meshe goes into a rant showing that she has been
forced into isolation, is caged and hungry. Tourists at the zoo stop for
a moment to stare at Meshe then move on to the next zoo animal.*

MESHE:
   Die-a-tribe! Yeah, so my tribe died — who cares! I don't wanta
   know about it. I wanta find them instead. I know they're extinct
   ... plus you can't smell them — the original wild herds. The
   wild ones were my cousins.

*The bison starts to chew her cud and sees Jesse and Lucie
approach. Meshe bellows loudly.*

JESSE:
   Hey, check out the buffalo, Lucie! *(taking out a cigarette)*

LUCIE:
   Yeah — what's with the muddy cud. Don't they eat grass? *(Jesse
   lights a cigarette)* No smoking, Jesse, we'll get kicked out.

*Meshe uses her horns and tries to smash the fence. The tourists run.
Jesse drops his cigarette which is interpreted as a tobacco offering
by Meshe.*

JESSE:

Whatever! Look at him. Looks totally out of its habitat.

MESHE:

Totally, and it's Me-*She*, not *He*!

JESSE:

What the —

MESHE:

Kinistitoh nah? (You understand?) It's Anishnaabe. It means I got a beard of grass but I'm still a matriarch. Something like that. Anyways, it's been awhile since neechies have visited this zoo. Maybe at Christmas time when it's all lit up here, every single tree. But they don't get out of their cars.

JESSE:

Did that buffalo just speak to us and call us neechies?

LUCIE:

I think so but could she —

MESHE:

Yes I did! And it's called a diatribe. And now I'll have another one … or maybe I just did a little one. Anyways, we have something in common, you were a dying tribe and so was I — Me-She. Matriarch — non ben (of all times) … okay.

They move in closer.

JESSE:

Cool.

LUCIE:

But how?

MESHE:

The cigarette — aren't you Cree?

LUCIE:

What?!

JESSE:

No way!

MESHE:

Get me outta here! I just had this vision of my relations. They
were in deep combat, going head to head — fighting over me. I
want away from this forest zoo!!

JESSE:

What the —

LUCIE:

— hell!

MESHE:

Would you live here? Don't be like typical tourists — please —
get me out of here.

They move in closer again.

JESSE:

Where would we take you?

MESHE:

To the water.

LUCIE:

You mean the river water?

MESHE:

(nods) There I can tell which way my herd went. You know, by looking at the flow of the river.

LUCIE:

This brochure says that the river only flows one way.

MESHE:

Hoofprints. I'll know from their hoofprints.

JESSE:

How will we get you out? What if we get caught? My year will be blown by Principal Dickason if I miss school one more time.

MESHE:

I need to get back to my herd — it's right behind a place called Wanuskewin — that way (points with her lips) I think. I need to wallow. I need to have a calf — I need to keep my line going. I like having a lot of lines. Especially as a buffalo. I need to be with my herd. What am I doing here? I mean, would you want to live here? Alone. I need my own kind.

LUCIE:

Does the zoo know you talk?

JESSE:

Yeah, that might have something to do with why you're here!

MESHE:

No.

Meshe then jumps over the fence to their astonishment.

JESSE:

Cha! Why didn't you do that before?!

LUCIE:
Yeah, you don't need us! You need a circus.

MESHE:
It's time! I heard my herd go by last night. There's something about you two. *(she moves in closer to them and studies their faces; the overcast skies look gloomy)* I was thinking perhaps if you disguised me as a fellow tourist no one will really know me at the main gate. Just get me through Sutherland residential area to the open fields by the river and I'll return your time.

Lucie and Jesse look at each other and agree. Lucie opens the picnic basket and together they disguise the enormous Meshe with a kerchief and a blanket. They are pleased with their work.

JESSE:
Alright.

LUCIE:
But just to the water. We gotta meet up with our school bus soon in the parking lot.

Thunderclap. They have reached the main gate of the zoo's parking lot and Meshe can see the open fields, knowing the river is just beyond. Suddenly the same Zookeeper comes up behind them.

ZOOKEEPER:
Wait a minute. Where you going?

JESSE:
What?! What buffalo?!

ZOOKEEPER:
You want to drive away now?! It's a threatening sky — gonna rain buckets any minute looks like — safer to hold up half an hour?!

LUCIE:
Oh? Well … we like the rain. It cleans our car.

JESSE:
Yeah, and it's a rental.

LUCIE:
You're no help.

ZOOKEEPER:
Okay, have a good day. You come back again.

MESHE:
Doubt it.

ZOOKEEPER:
I beg your pardon —

JESSE:
No doubt about it.

MESHE:
At last — yes!

Meshe is just about to reach the grassy field and anticipates sinking her hooves into a familiar habitat.

ZOOKEEPER:
What — hey?! Do I know her?

JESSE:
No. She's old.

LUCIE:
Thanks. Thank you.

They exit the zoo gate nonchalantly, then flee. Exeunt.

*Lighting comes up intensely on Dr. Palen back at his lecture,
downstage center. Dr. Palen unfreezes.*

DR. PALEN:
>   The bison to cross Beringia were not the first to do so, a million
>   years ago, the Leptobos — a primitive cow-family line were
>   here but couldn't acclimatize to the north. These first bison
>   were small-bodied, small-horned, fast-moving dwellers of
>   forest edges and meadows. They were wiped out. Bull. There
>   was no record of bulls either. Could be why this line died out —
>   hey guys?! The more durable line for the northern climate came
>   next. The bison B. priscus. They existed six-hundred thousand
>   years ago, and as recently as three-hundred thousand years ago.
>   Other grazers of this period were ... woolly mammoths and
>   horses. Fascinating, right?!

*Dr. Palen freezes as a dance of birth begins. Light fades and comes
up on another part of the stage.*

*The setting is an open prairie field of long green grasses and the
occasional patch of wildflowers, first yellow then purple. A buffalo
cow gives birth — the calf is a bright red-rust color. The new calf,
Rusty, begins a frantic struggle to get to her feet. She gets halfway
up several times and falls forward, backward, and sideways. Finally
the calf staggers with her weak young legs and runs away.*

*Predator music is introduced. A wolf is seen in the distance. He
approaches, so the mother gets the young one to run. The mother
bison is captured. The wolf devours her. Mother has sacrificed her
life for her newborn. The wolf then takes off.*

*Rusty, the newborn calf, runs about chaotically once she notices her
mother's body. Lucie, Jesse, and Meshe re-enter.*

LUCIE:

Lookit this little one, Jess? Awww, ever cute!

Rusty runs right up beside Jesse and stops.

JESSE:

What am I, a buffalo magnet?!

LUCIE:

Meshe, what're we gonna do with this rusty little guy?

MESHE:

Looks like she's coming along. Maybe she can lead us to the herd.

RUSTY:

Tantae to tayeen? (Where we going?)

MESHE:

To the river. Teach you to swim.

Dr. Palen unfreezes again.

DR. PALEN:

Survival. Bison regurgitate their cud. Now filled with bacteria. Assists their food digestion. But why am I talking about the stomach?! Bison B. priscus did produce some offshoots. B. latifrons — stood some twenty percent taller — their bony horns spanned six feet! B. latifrons weighed three thousand pounds and appeared three-hundred thousand years ago. Did you know excavation unearthed a B. latifrons in downtown San Francisco that lived there only twenty-five thousand years ago? They're getting closer and closer to us, aren't they? *(he picks up two sticks lying on the ground and holds them to his head like horns)* After B. latifrons came B. antiquus. They were smaller bodied and much smaller horned. *(he snaps a horn for emphasis)* Oops! *(snaps the other horn but it too has snapped short)* Oh well. *(Palen then holds the horns up to his ears and walks around, mimicking a B. antiquus bison)* But what happened to B. antiquus? *(throws the horns down)* They disappeared! — about twelve thousand years later. B. antiquus was replaced by B. occidentalis. Again a smaller bison. All born of the bison B. priscus line still occupying what was called the Mammoth Steppe or if you will — one step for mankind, a mammoth steppe for all buffalo. I digress — this one time I thought I saw a real ancient bison in the present day, I could tell from their hooves and eyes. But where was I? Yes, over here. With its horns pointed up, parallel to the plane of its face from nose to forehead — kinda like Celine Dion — like this. Feel free to take a picture anytime, you're never going to see this again, let me tell you. I'm as close as you get. Where the B. antiquus died out everywhere B. occidentalis had an even shorter life as a species.

Dr. Palen places his hat over his heart as he exits.

Meshe, Jess, Lucie, and Rusty are at the river's edge. A gigantic splash is heard and the sound of a buffalo herd.

MESHE:
   Hear that?!

LUCIE:
   Sounds like thunder!

MESHE:
   That's my herd!

LUCIE:
   I don't see buffalo. Where's the sound coming from?

JESSE:

Look, their tracks stop at the edge here.

MESHE:

They swam across.

JESSE:

You don't want to swim across *that* river!?

LUCIE:

I know!

RUSTY:

Do I have to swim?

MESHE:

You, little one, were swimming for months before you were born.

RUSTY:

Really, I don't remember that, all I know is the wolf ate my mom so he wouldn't eat me.

MESHE:

Let me remind you! *(pushes Rusty into the river)* Come on, don't stop moving your legs, head up!

LUCIE:

I see tracks going in but I don't see anything coming out the other side!

The buffalo, Lucie, and Jesse swim across the river.

Dr. Palen re-enters, lecturing.

DR. PALEN:

>Five thousand years ago B. occidentalis was replaced by B. bison. B. bison changed little for at least a quarter million years. But changed a great deal during the last ten thousand years. B. bison endured. Horses, camels, mammoths, mastodons all vanished from around the prairies but not the B. bison. Why?!

Dr. Palen exits searching for his answer.

Meshe, Jesse, Lucie, and Rusty reach the other side of the river. Jesse and Lucie have now transformed into buffalo.

JESSE BUFFALO:

>Lookit — we're buffalo!

LUCIE BUFFALO:

>Suddenly I feel I could eat a whole field of grass.

JESSE BUFFALO:

>How did this happen, Meshe?

LUCIE BUFFALO:

>Hey, I'm all legs now.

Rusty approaches Meshe and the new buffalo.

MESHE:

>See it's time for the buffalo to return. Welcome to my herd. Rusty, come here and receive our new members with me.

RUSTY:

>How come they get to be so big if they're so new?

JESSE BUFFALO:

>Meshe, are we the buffalo you were looking for?

The four buffalo have been roaming and come upon a butte.

MESHE:
> Buffalo Butte?!! See this rock, that's what brought you back.

JESSE BUFFALO:
> Yeah?

LUCIE BUFFALO:
> Really?!

MESHE:
> You want to know the story of the birth of the original buffalo?
> Sounds like a trick question coming from a buffalo. Long
> ago, right after the beginning of time, there were mountains
> everywhere. Way in the west lives an old buffalo mountain. One
> night a giant meteor fell upon the prairie, splatting the mountain
> flat with her caught underneath. And the spirits saw this prairie
> being created from where they perched on top. Spring would
> come, the ice would melt, and suddenly the water flowed,
> gushing out of the mountain top, covering the world of prairie.
> And that buffalo, still flattened deep under the water, broke the
> surface, so huge was she that suddenly the water became rivers.
> North and South Saskatchewan. Not sure if ground would hold
> her massive frame, she knelt down to birth a herd of buffalos.
> She then froze again, sunk and became a large rock. The land
> around her is called — Ka-tep-wa?!! (Who calls?) *(her voice
> reverberates into a whispering echo of Katepwa amplified in
> soundscape.)* Qu-Apelle? Echo. Hear it? That's our vibration.

Jesse Buffalo exits.

*The remaining herd begins a comic Cow to Cow Dance. They move
together, heads all pointing the same way. One cow pauses to lick a
ticklish rib and then looks around mischievously. Her companions*

bump into each other; still, they are alert to predators, but for a second. The old cow is belligerent, forcing the others to be serious by swinging her horns and lunging. This pressure makes subordinates obey. Then there is competition for food, wallows, and water. All jockey for position whatever they do. They are like a bunch of old ladies crashing the door to the opening of a monster bingo. They exit.

Dr. Palen re-enters.

DR. PALEN:
Why! Let me tell you why!! The "Pleistocene Overkill Hypothesis." That's why! Climate changed rapidly as the last ice age ended. We no longer had summer rainfall. All grasses dependent on that rainfall died out. Habitat change gave some species the axe. The rope. The bullet. The slit to the throat. The bomb. Die already! Then there was mankind himself, with the bladed spear — hunters. The bison determined that to stand and fight was a much riskier strategy with this new predator. Those who lived by the spear died by the spirit. Today there's a division — B. bison athabascae or wood bison. Elsewhere it is the B. bison bison or plains bison.

All the buffalo move in slowly to surround and corral Dr. Palen.

DR. PALEN:
This made running away their mode of choice. Hehe —

MESHE:
Excuse me!

DR. PALEN:
(startled) Yes.

MESHE:
The buffalo was a hybrid.

DR. PALEN:

Hybrid?

MESHE:

Hybrid, it's a combination of two animals.

DR. PALEN:

I know what hybrid means — which two?

MESHE:

Indians made two extinct ones into a new one, that's how.
Didn't you ever wonder why we survived when there's no
book? We came close to extermination just like the red man.
Now we're both flourishing in numbers.

DR. PALEN:

Yes, we must praise the field park workers and a few generous
citizens — I mean foundations. In the case of reversing the
threat of extinction — for the bison, I mean.

MESHE:

Well who cares who it was done for — we helped each other
while the white man tried to get us all! That's not right. Did you
ever consider that we had a special bond with the human? If
they got nothing to eat they starve and die. You know all about
habitat change.

DR. PALEN:

As a matter of fact I do. Now in terms of —

MESHE:

Scientists! *(pause)* You named us bison. The French called us
Les Boeufs and that became buffalo. But that's okay, you got to
call us something to prove we exist.

DR. PALEN:
    Your point is?

MESHE:
    We purposely survived.

DR. PALEN:
    There is something called carrying weight. I do not believe
    the sole purpose of the extermination threat was completely
    intended to —

MESHE:
    You do not believe in much ... other than your science.

DR. PALEN:
    Don't talk to me anymore, it's not natural for bison to talk.

MESHE:
    Who says buffalo talk?

Meshe starts to sing a healing song.

RUSTY/JESSE/LUCIE BUFFALO:
    We're not talking.

The buffalo turn their backs on Dr. Palen and begin to desert him.

DR. PALEN:
    No wait! Please! Don't go, I am ... buffalo — come back. I cried
    so hard as a kid, I wanted to fit in, I wanted to be free, I wanted
    to be one of you so bad and I was for a long time. Then I grew up
    not knowing who I was until I was studying you.

*Dr. Palen is in a trance, as if from the power of the healing song
which tugs at his spirit to join them. The buffalo circle him as he*

crumbles. They disrobe Dr. Palen and robe him again so he is transformed into an elder buffalo. We hear his protest quips and acceptance: "Hey! Ouch, easy now!" "Not there that tickles!" "Hee hee — ohh my ..." He rises.

RUSTY:
Wenesh keen? (Who are you now?)

DR. PALEN (now GRANDFATHER BUFFALO):
Grand Herd Leader!

RUSTY:
I'm of the Meshe matriarchs.

MESHE:
Yes.

GRANDFATHER BUFFALO:
And you?

LUCIE BUFFALO:
I'm just a Plain ole buffalo.

GRANDFATHER BUFFALO:
Then you must be —

JESSE BUFFALO:
Wood.

GRANDFATHER BUFFALO:
I figured. Are you family?

ALL:
Yes!!! 'Cause we're Rock.

MESHE:

They came from this rock over here.

JESSE BUFFALO:

I'm the first born — Mudjeekwis.

LUCIE BUFFALO:

No, I was born first — we're twins, remember.

MESHE:

I was going to tell you — buffalo don't birth twins — you're related but probably cousins. You had to be raised together — remember survival. It's been chaos.

GRANDFATHER BUFFALO:

Family was a pretty big thing back then.

LUCIE BUFFALO:

Seventy-five or so —

JESSE BUFFALO:

Million!

RUSTY:

(to Grandfather Buffalo) That's big! That's real big — you know numbers — that's pretty big!

MESHE:

We don't roam together anymore. But the young ones, the old ones all have to come together. This is the time. There's a balance that must take place.

GRANDFATHER BUFFALO:

I didn't tell you my other name. It's Moshum noosim.

JESSE BUFFALO:
Does that mean I'm really your grandson? Wow, I thought I didn't have a grandfather.

GRANDFATHER BUFFALO:
Yes, and it means I'm part human, like all buffalo are. You know that.

LUCIE BUFFALO:
You don't look like a human buffalo to me.

GRANDFATHER BUFFALO:
You don't have to look like one to be one.

RUSTY:
Yes you do.

GRANDFATHER BUFFALO:
Funny coming from a buffalo looking like you.

RUSTY:
I was born this way.

Rusty stamps her hooves and exits exasperated.

MESHE:
I remember this one story how we came out of the water. The old ones say that when the killings began, some buffalo fled back to the water, purposely drowning themselves to go back to that large rock. The rock that birthed us. Man made a dam bigger than the beaver and covered it. This rock. One day in the future the buffalo shall return in great glory to its original people. They were the buffalo at one time a long time ago. They came from beneath this large rock.

She sings a buffalo memorial song before the giant rock butte.

JESSE BUFFALO:
> *(to the rock)* So this is the rock!

LUCIE BUFFALO:
> *(to Grandfather Buffalo)* Told you we Rock.

Meshe is now frozen.

JESSE BUFFALO:
> Hey! Auntie, can you hear me? It's like she doesn't know we're here!

MESHE:
> *(still in a trance; voice of an ancient)* We must in our lifetime have as many calves as we can.

LUCIE BUFFALO:
> With more than one bull? Ouch!

MESHE:
> Settle down.

JESSE BUFFALO:
> Meshe, are you scared for us, you know, as a species?

MESHE:
> Yes, we're running out of time.

LUCIE BUFFALO:
> How come?

MESHE:
> Mothers aren't mating. It's dry, we need water.

Rusty enters, she has transformed into a White Buffalo Calf.

LUCIE BUFFALO:
Rusty, I never noticed until now but you look kinda albino.

JESSE BUFFALO:
A white buffalo. Yeah right?!!

GRANDFATHER BUFFALO:
She has brown eyes. Albinos have red eyes. But there's something else about her.

WHITE BUFFALO CALF:
Oh yeah, I have turned white!

Meshe snaps out of her trance.

MESHE:
So the White Buffalo Calf has arrived. We've been waiting a long time for you. *(pause)* We have to keep moving.

They come upon a cattle guard.

WHITE BUFFALO CALF:
What is this?!!!

LUCIE BUFFALO:
It's called a cattle guard.

MESHE:
The land has been cut up. Our traditional route is gone.

LUCIE BUFFALO:
Cattle guard can't stop us — doesn't need to stop us.

Grandfather Buffalo places his hooves on the narrow bars of the
cattle guard and dances on his tiptoes all the way across. Each
follows with their individual ritual dance of crossing the threshold to
freedom. Each celebrate their success and roam free.

The soundscore changes to a strutting pulsing beat. This sets up the
four buffalo into a Dance of Breeding:
A female bison (Meshe) spies an attractive bull (Grand Herd Leader).
She breaks away from a tending bull (Jesse Buffalo).
She runs through the herd, as if attracting a string of bulls.
The other cows wallow (White Buffalo Calf and Lucie Buffalo),
while she puts her horn in his ribs, he grunts.
She is ready and tries to mount him.
He gets the message and circles, she raises her tail and braces her hooves.
The bull mounts, mating is quick.
The bull retreats to the herd's side.
She is wobbly and staggers a few steps. She is done for the season.
No more male advances are accepted.

The soundscore switches to nature sounds of summer moving into
fall. All the buffalo participate in the daily herd activities as we
witness a choreographed Dance of Summer and Fall:
Grazing as much as they can with as little exercise as possible — it is
energy building time.
Danger of midsummer, potential predator is false alarm.
One bull rises, stretches, stands.
Others follow.
Tension develops, again a predator is a mirage.
Bodies stiffen, tails which had been flicking flies are still.
A stare-off.
Slowly they relax.
One buffalo lies down, the others join.

WHITE BUFFALO CALF:
>What are yous up to?!

GRANDFATHER BUFFALO:
>Getting fat.

MESHE:
>We're doing nothing.

GRANDFATHER BUFFALO:
>Exactly. If you do nothing you get fat.

WHITE BUFFALO CALF:
>You want to get fat?!

GRANDFATHER BUFFALO:
>Yes. Right after breeding season. We have to put on fat for the long harsh winter. Fat is energy. Fat is survival.

LUCIE BUFFALO:
>Survival fat.

GRANDFATHER BUFFALO:
>The fastest way to the goal, not rushing anything! To stillness.

JESSE BUFFALO:
>To statues.

A blanket of snow covers the playspace supported by the soundscape of a prairie winter.

All the buffalo engage in a Dance of Winter:
A slow-motion sequence as food is scarce through long winter months. The buffalo sweep the snow by swinging their heads from side to side. Using their muzzles as plows they clear little craters in the snow

*and eat the grass at the bottom. They all become covered in white,
and are shivering until they freeze to form a herd statue.*

Finally the Sun returns.

*A Dance for Spring:
Restores their energy, the buffalo statues slowly come alive.
With sun on their faces, the buffalo stretch to wake up and stand to
raise their front hooves to the sun, pulling the sun to their faces with
a small bounce. They turn bouncing, pulling the sun energy towards
them, until they all meet in the middle and spread out to herd
positions where each takes a turn leading the herd's spring ritual
awakening. It's a dance celebrating new life.*

*A Fight Dance, Bull to Bull (with a rapid percussive soundscore
which builds in intensity):
Two bulls wallow then tear the sod with their horns and create dust.
The fighting bulls plow the soil with their hooves.
They slam heads, the shock explodes dust from their bodies.
The old bull bellows. Back arches, belly lifts, neck extends,
     a lion-like roar erupts, then he charges again.
The six-year-old bull bellows back.
And heads to the old bull ...menacingly.
His forefeet stamp with each step. He snorts.
The old bull, not intimidated, advances, matching stamp for stamp.
Snort with snort.
Bellows intensify, pure fury. Locking of horns. Hooking uppercuts.
Shoving head to head.
Impact so hard the old bull is flipped over in a somersault.
He rises, they then circle each other.
Head to head blows.
All of a sudden — they withdraw.
And circle again.
Now head to head combat.
One submits.*

Shows vulnerability and turns away.
A swing of the head.
A horn in ribcage causing a deep gash; he doesn't recover this time.
The young bull lunges in and strikes again. The old bull retreats to die.
The survivor runs.

WHITE BUFFALO CALF:
> Grandfather?!

GRANDFATHER BUFFALO:
> He got me.

WHITE BUFFALO CALF:
> No, you're just hurt bad — let me help!

GRANDFATHER BUFFALO:
> No — not this time — I'm afraid my time is up, Little One. You
> run with the herd — go now — this is your chance before they
> disappear. I leave happy knowing I die a buffalo.

WHITE BUFFALO CALF:
> Moshum, tell me the story of the White Buffalo Calf-Woman —
> and how she arrived with a pipe.

GRANDFATHER BUFFALO:
> How she was beautiful to look at and one warrior had bad
> thoughts and then a black cloud came over him and turned him
> into a skeleton.

WHITE BUFFALO CALF:
> She told the people about the buffalo. Because they were
> starving she turned herself into a white buffalo calf. And right
> after there were herds and herds of buffalo — for miles! Like
> ten or twenty miles of nothing but a sea of buffalo.

GRANDFATHER BUFFALO:
> That's right, my girl! That's right. Once we were many. We
> were the moving water above the ground.

He dies.

WHITE BUFFALO CALF:
> She'll return someday for the sacred bundle. When there is the
> birth of a white buffalo calf, that's happened. Moshum, where's
> the bundle? You didn't tell me where to look?!!!

*Grandfather Buffalo reappears now as a spirit. A large stuffed
buffalo is revealed beneath the butte set piece.*

GRANDFATHER BUFFALO:
> The sacred bundle is in you my girl — now is your time.

WHITE BUFFALO CALF:
> Moshum?! Time — my time for what?!

GRANDFATHER BUFFALO:
> For the Earth to heal. Last chance and for all people. We belong
> to society. Strong as we can make it. Strong as we can take
> them. *(in Cree)* Look ahead Noosim, go forward. Wechee ge
> wagu-magunuk. (All my relations.)

*White Buffalo Calf then places a buffalo robe upon him and covers
his body. His spirit now joins other buffalo spirits who sing an
honor song for his passing. They remove their buffalo headpieces
and place them in a pile then dance a circle around him. Buffalo
Jesse leads the song with a hand-drum, the others carry rattles,
in respect of all buffalo passing. The stuffed buffalo is imposing
as it stands proudly behind everyone under a bright spotlight that
dims just as you think you see its eyes move. The lighting fades and
comes up on another part of the stage.*

Jesse and Lucie return back to the zoo as humans again.

JESSE:
> Hey, we're no longer buffalo!

LUCIE:
> Oh yeah!

JESSE:
> Where did we go? Was I hallucinating?

LUCIE:
> No, we were buffalo.

JESSE:
> Yes — we went back, eh?

LUCIE:
> Back to the herd?

JESSE:
> Yeah.

He tries some buffalo moves.

LUCIE:
> Found your inner buffalo?

JESSE:
> I did.

LUCIE:
> When can we go back?

JESSE:

I don't think we can.

LUCIE:

Why?

JESSE:

'Cause.

LUCIE:

'Cause why, Jesse? I want to go back there, it was comfortable.
I felt Mom.

JESSE:

'Cause we've been shown what to do here, Meshe said —

LUCIE:

I gotta find out more about that White Buffalo Calf-Woman!

JESSE:

Meshe said it, sister.

LUCIE:

But I'm not your sister ... am I? We returned but where is she?

JESSE:

Come on, we better find our class.

LUCIE:

We can't leave without saying thank you to Meshe.

JESSE:

Alright then, let's go see if she's still at the zoo cage.

LUCIE:

> *(they see the buffalo statue)* That's not Meshe. The zoo must
> have put a stuffed one in her place. *(stands in front of Meshe's
> fenced lot)* Awww! Lookit the baby buffalo over there! Her
> name is Mudblanket.

JESSE:

> Come on — let's bounce. Don't wanta miss the school bus.

They exit past the empty zoo fence.

Curtain.

END OF PLAY